SMALL APAR+MEN+S

A NOVEL BY CHRIS MILLIS

anvil
PRESS

Second Edition: August, 2013

Printed and bound in Canada
Cover Image: Courtesy of Silver Nitrate Films
Author photo: Mandy Dennis

Canadian Cataloguing in Publication Data

Millis, Christopher

    Small apartments / Christopher Millis. -- New format ed.

    ISBN 978-1-927380-63-5

I. Title
PS3613.I54S62 2013   813.'6   C2013-911579-X

Represented in Canada by Publishers Group Canada (PGC)
Distributed by Raincoast Distribution

The publisher gratefully acknowledges the financial assistance of the B.C. Arts Council, the Canada Council for the Arts, and the Canada Book Fund for their support of our publishing program.

Anvil Press
P.O. Box 3008, Main Post Office
Vancouver, B.C. V6B 3X5 Canada
www.anvilpress.com

Apartments are like bowling shoes,
Small compartments for us to use.
One removes us from the rain,
The other improves our bowling game.

For Lisa

I wish to thank my friends and family who have always
supported me in all my creative endeavours.

And thanks to the staff at Anvil Press.

1

F ACE UP AND smiling lay the warm, dead body of Albert Olivetti on the cracked, linoleum kitchenette floor of Franklin's small apartment on the west side of Buffalo.

With a butter knife, Franklin tore open an envelope from the previous day's mail and read the brief note scrawled onto the back of a Wal-Mart receipt for a hand-held tape recorder. It was Tuesday.

The note said: There are more where these came from.

Franklin tapped three fingernail clippings onto the lonely, simulated-wood table by the window of his apartment. It was another bizarre missive from his brother Bernard, who was crazy. There are more where these came from indeed, thought Franklin. But for how long? How did Bernard replenish his nails so quickly? His personal supply must be near exhaustion.

Three mailings per week made nine nails. Where did Bernard get all the money for postage? Did they have a postal desk at the psychiatric hospital where he was a resident?

Franklin wondered if Bernard sent fingernails only to his brother. Perhaps there were others. Perhaps Bernard sent envelopes stuffed with fingernails and strange messages to his first love, Rebecca DeLeggio, from Miss Parson's class at Grover Cleveland Elementary. What would prevent him from sending them to the clean-shaven, bald man with the profound stutter at the Rent-A-Centre on Hertel Avenue? Or even to the President of the United States, Himself.

Franklin sat in his underwear and wondered. His ample white belly spilled over his Fruit of the Loom waistband. He poked it and it jiggled. Franklin chuckled to himself.

Franklin assumed that he was the only one who received fingernail clippings and notes from his brother Bernard. But one must never assume, he thought. He was reminded of the ·lesson drummed into his brain in Miss Parson's class. She would stand at the head of the class, her head like a wrinkled grape placed atop a stiff wool dress, and spell "ASSUME" on the blackboard, which was really green. She then circled three separate bits to make her point.

"When you ASSUME," Miss Parson would say, waiting a beat for the class to drone out the refrain, "you make an 'ASS' out of 'U' and 'ME'."

"That is correct," said Miss Parson.

FRANKLIN'S HOUND DOG bit furiously at its ass.

Franklin heaved a heavy sigh, causing his white belly to

quiver. His brother Bernard was insane. This was a fact, not an assumption. Franklin carefully replaced the clippings and the cryptic note and placed the envelope with the others.

Outside his only window, which was between the kitchenette and the living room, Franklin could see bits of his neighbourhood on Buffalo's west side. It was late August and the leaves on the maple tree outside Franklin's window were beginning to turn orange and red. Soon they would wilt and fall, giving Franklin a clearer view of the yellow building across the street where the pretty single mother and her daughter lived. The daughter was no more than fifteen, Franklin assumed (there was that word again), and the mother barely twice her age. Oh, how Franklin had lusted over those luscious ladies these last four years. Franklin had traveled around the world and back again with both of them, though they never knew it. For instance, Sunday afternoon, moments after they unloaded the groceries in front of their building, they were both in the bubble bath with Franklin, slipping and sliding and satisfying him, and each other. At least that's how Franklin remembered it.

Franklin lived at 100 Garner. His building was slate grey with a rusty, red trim. There were three apartments, two on the first floor and one upper. The first floor studio belonged to Franklin and the one-bedroom next door was occupied by the irascible Mr. Allspice. The upstairs unit was another one-bedroom rented by a twenty-four-year-old pothead who called himself Tommy Balls. Franklin did not know the names of the girls across the street, so he called them 101 and Little 101 because that was the address nailed beside their door. Of course he never had occasion to call them anything, their names were exclusively for his own silent reference. Staring absent-mindedly at the numbers on the side of their yellow building made Franklin remember his visit downtown four years ago to the Department of Motor Vehicles. He handed his form to the young woman behind the counter with earrings in her ears, nose, eyebrow and, as Franklin was about to discover, her tongue. She looked over the application and said, "Is that Street, Avenue, what?"

"Huh?" muttered Franklin.

"On your application here for a driver's license," said the perforated state worker. "You wrote just 100 Garner on your form for street address. Is that 100 Garner Street, 100 Garner Avenue...what is it?"

"I don't know. It just says Garner."

"Where?"

"Where what?" replied Franklin.

"Where does it just say Garner, fool!" barked the young woman, flashing her studded tongue.

"On the sign," said Franklin. He looked around behind him to the weary souls in line and gave them an expression that said, That was an easy one.

The young woman, ignoring Franklin's victory smirk, took a black BiC medium round stic disposable pen from behind her ear and wrote "Street" on the address line after the word "Garner."

Franklin had lived at 100 Garner—now 100 Garner Street—for four years. Before that he had lived with his brother Bernard, who was now officially crazy, for twenty-two years at 57 Ashland. Not Street or Avenue, just 57 Ashland. For all that time Franklin had never needed a driver's license. It just never came up. But now that Bernard was crazy, Franklin was responsible for driving his own fat ass around Buffalo.

Back in 1A, Franklin's first floor studio apartment at 100 Garner Street, the dog yawned. It was almost noon. Time for Franklin to turn his energies towards a much happier pursuit, his music. As he padded barefoot across the apartment, his belly swam back and forth, challenging the integrity of his elastic waistband. He picked up his alphorn, closed his eyes, inhaled deeply—his circumference expanding to a freakish degree—and blew. He blew a long, low eerie note. The dog howled as the apartment began to melt away like a ten-cent candle.

Franklin re-opened his eyes beneath the crisp blue skies of Switzerland. He stood atop a green, grassy hill in only his white underpants. The Nordic wind parted his hairy back. A flock of California condors, unique to Switzerland, sliced the air above Franklin's head. The birds cast a long, v-shaped shadow which Franklin and his mighty horn stood at the centre of.

Picture frames on the wall began to rattle. Franklin's teacup danced in its saucer as the boorish thumping of Mr. Allspice in 2A shattered Franklin's vision.

"This is a residential neighbourhood you fat twit!" screamed Mr. Allspice. "I'm going to screw that horn into your fat ass!"

The cries from next door were muffled, but Franklin could hear them plainly enough. He set down the horn. Better to lay low, he thought, especially with the dead body in the kitchenette. He returned to his chair by the window and rubbed the throbbing bump on his head. He had banged it with such force that morning that it was now swollen and tender. When he ran his fingertips over the bruise it felt like his skull had bubbled up. I should ice this bump, he thought. He shuffled over to the icebox and removed a plastic tray—empty. He filled it at the sink, replaced it in the freezer, and returned to his aluminum-framed utility chair with the hard orange vinyl-covered seat and back. The small chair, with its skinny metal legs, looked incapable of supporting his gooey, 235-pound, 5'5" anatomy.

I need to get out of here, Franklin thought as he again stared at the yellow building across the street. Out of this small apartment and away from this crummy city. He twisted his pinky finger into his left ear as his thoughts returned to his brother.

Apparently, Bernard had not always been crazy. He earned his Master's Degree from the University of Buffalo and worked as an accountant for a successful downtown law firm named Weiner and Fish. Bernard's skin was the colour of communion wine. His suits appeared more expensive than they were because they were tailored to fit like a second skin. His ties were silk and monochromatic, green was his favourite—it matched his bottle-green eyes. He was 6'3", 185 lbs., with ink-black hair that he grew long and thick so he could comb it straight back with a smear of pomade. Bernard had come home to 57 Ashland with a crew cut the day before he checked himself into the Buffalo Psychiatric Center on Elmwood Avenue. As far as Franklin knew, his brother still had the same haircut.

Bernard brought home a parade of girlfriends. He would usually take them bowling on a first date. Bernard carried a 160 average, but he would sandbag for the girls. Bernard did not put on airs. He did not care what impressed a woman. "Take them bowling," Bernard would say. "That's how you flush out the tight-asses. Uptight chicks refuse to bowl. And if they won't bowl, they won't roll. If you know what I mean."

Franklin was pretty sure he knew what he meant. But not positive.

Bernard brought home many girls but Franklin had his favourites. Frieda had wild, curly red hair. She worked as a waitress in a Greek diner in Allentown. She would sit on the carpet and paint her toenails while the three of them watched rented movies on Friday nights. The smell of the nail polish gave Franklin a headache but he would never ask Frieda to stop. He adored her bony feet from his dark chair in the corner. "Can you see the TV all right, sugar?" Frieda would ask. "I can see everything just fine," said Franklin.

Becca was a short, thin yenta from Suffolk County with spindly legs and freakishly large breasts. She talked and talked, never seeming to require oxygen. It was as if she possessed an internal breathing apparatus that rendered inhalation superfluous. Franklin was fascinated by the foreign cadence of her Long Island dialect. He also liked that she called him Boobala. He didn't know what Boobala meant, but he would have handed her twenty bucks every time she said it.

There were others, too. Andrea: the yoga instructor from Williamsville; Sarah: the jet engine mechanic from Tonawanda; the other Sarah: the peppy and athletic University of Buffalo senior who was captain of her lacrosse team. Franklin enjoyed the glimpses he got into these girls' lives: the offhanded snatches of conversation which revealed one to be "on the pill," or another as "constantly horny." Bernard's girlfriends would always chat freely with Franklin while his brother was en route from work, or in his bedroom dressing and applying a liberal coating of musk.

Before he checked himself into a mental hospital, Bernard drove a maroon 1994 Mazda 626 four-door with standard transmission and a six-cylinder engine. Bernard used to drive Franklin all over Buffalo. He would drive Franklin anywhere he needed, or wanted, to go. He drove him to the flea market on Military Avenue the Saturday five years earlier when Franklin decided to buy an alphorn from a skinny old man wearing a short-brimmed straw hat with a loud, floral band.

"You know what that is, son?" the man in the unfortunate hat asked Franklin that Saturday afternoon. Franklin was fingering the horn as it leaned against a fold-out card table with a colour ad for Lucky Strike cigarettes pasted to its top. "That is a gen-u-ine, goddamn alphorn."

"Is it from Switzerland?" asked Franklin.

"Why, you bet your sweet balls it is."

Franklin paid the man $200 of Bernard's money for the horn without dickering. As he and Bernard drove home to 57 Ashland they had to leave the back window rolled down with the skinny end of the horn sticking out because it was too long to fit in the Mazda. Bernard thought Franklin was crazy for buying an alphorn that day. How about that? thought Franklin as he sat on his orange utility chair inside 100 Garner sipping cold tea. It was less than a year from the day when the now famous self-help author and Guru of Mental Fitness, Dr. Sage Mennox, personally diagnosed Bernard as "Nuts." Dr. Mennox said that without immediate psychiatric care, Bernard would be "miles and miles down the Road to Crazy."

FRANKLIN GLANCED DOWN at Mr. Olivetti sprawled out and smiling on the pale yellow, cracked linoleum floor. He rested his flabby elbows on his fat kneecaps and stared at the body. Mr. Olivetti's head was upside down from Franklin's perspective and resting between Franklin's bare feet. What a look Mr. Olivetti had on his face. His eyes were wide open and his mouth was bent into the corniest grin. This old ginny looks like he just won a free trip, thought Franklin. I guess he has.

"Where the hell did Bernard get a Wal-Mart receipt for a hand-held tape recorder?" Franklin asked Mr. Olivetti.

Franklin poured out the rest of his Moxie trying to aim it into Mr. Olivetti's frozen smile, but he missed. Franklin was never good at those kinds of things, things that required skill and a steady hand. He sat back in his chair and stared at the dead flies inside the fluorescent light on the ceiling.

"This apartment is too small for me," Franklin told Mr. Olivetti. "Do you know that I am destined for bigger and better things? My brother Bernard always told me that I'm special. 'You are special Franklin,' he would say. Maybe I should just leave Buffalo. I'll bet you'd like that, wouldn't you Mr. Olivetti? Maybe I'll just go someplace where people respect me, and they're not so mean, and they appreciate my music. Someplace where there is no Mr.-fucking-Allspice in 2A banging on the walls. Someplace like Switzerland."

Switzerland. In every spare moment Franklin dreamed of Switzerland. It must be Utopia, he thought. A land of pastoral serenity where he would be free to lie naked in the tall grass beside an Alpine lake spooning with his mighty horn.

Franklin's dog sniffed Mr. Olivetti's face. He started to lick the Moxie from his cheek but balked at the bitter taste. Circling a spot on the floor, he flopped down beside the dead man and heaved a heavy sigh. He then began to lick himself with intense focus.

Dead flies. Dead Mr. Olivetti. Life is short and full of surprises, Franklin thought.

CHAP+ER

2

FRANKLIN'S UPSTAIRS NEIGHBOUR, Tommy Balls, was baked out of his gourd. Tommy's project for the day was to construct a device known as a "gravity bong." Tommy's best friend Tony, who was three credits away from an Associates Degree in Hotel Management at Erie Community College, had drawn a basic diagram on a cocktail napkin of the components required to make the bong and how those components must be arranged. Over a couple of beers at Mulligan's Brick Bar in Allentown, Tony gave Tommy Balls an enthusiastic testimonial on the gravity bong's advanced effects. They had just finished assaulting their eardrums for three hours across the street at Nietzsche's, with the four chords and confusing lyrics of the local band "Vomit." They could barely hear each other above the ringing.

"You're going to love this fucking gravity bong," said Tony.

"What?" shouted Tommy Balls.

"I said Fucking Gravity Bong, baby!"

"Yeah," agreed Tommy Balls.

Building the bong was Tommy Balls' project for Tuesday, but that is not to suggest that he was up and moving around his apartment. No, he was sitting on the faded green corduroy couch his parents let him have when he moved out six months ago. Tommy moved out voluntarily—and rather theatrically—after a poorly conceived, and badly delivered, drug-induced argument with his mother about the quality of her meatloaf. There were deeper issues, of course, and the meatloaf was just a catalyst. Tommy used the opportunity to deliver a fierce monologue on what he perceived to be his parents' shortcomings. His speech was so venomous that it made his mother dash into her bedroom crying. She spent the rest of the evening reading and scribbling notes inside the dust jackets of her Dr. Mennox books. His father, for his part, put on his hat and drove to the Knights of Columbus Hall. Within the week Tommy had put down a deposit on an apartment at 100 Garner.

TOMMY HAD JUST finished smoking a joint and was in a pleasant state between consciousness and sleep as he stared into the television. An episode of *Magnum, P.I.* was on. It was twenty-four minutes into a twelve-hour marathon.

As he gawked catatonically at the television, Tommy ran through his mind all the objects he would need to build his inaugural gravity bong. First he would need a bucket. He was pretty sure he had a bucket behind the door in the bathroom. He had a faint recollection of a white plastic bucket with one dark sock in it. Next he would need a two-litre plastic soda bottle. He would need to cut the bottom off of that, so he would also need a serrated knife and a pair of scissors. Tommy knew he had the knife, and probably the scissors, but he was positive he did not have the soda bottle. Although he consumed, on average, three cans of beer and one two-litre bottle of soda pop per day, he had just brought an entire month's worth (ninety-eight cans and thirty-three bottles) to the recycle machine at the Open 24 Hours convenience store where he was a clerk. He'd applied the resulting $6.55 towards the purchase of a dime bag from Bobo at the pool hall on Elmwood Avenue. Securing a soda pop bottle without making a trip to the 2-4 store may pose a problem, thought Tommy.

Finally, the gravity bong called for weed. He had plenty of that, thanks to Bobo. Tommy budgeted for two things in his life: rent and weed. I have to have weed and a place to smoke it, he reasoned. His job as a clerk at the 2-4 store on the corner of Grant Street and Forest Avenue allowed him to barely afford both.

Bucket. Knife. Scissors. Weed . . . soda pop bottle.

Tommy blinked and a glimmer of awareness, however faint, crept in behind his eyes. Tommy scratched at his orange goatee. He was positive there were no two-litre soda pop bottles within the confines of his apartment. He ran through his options. He could go purchase a two-litre beverage and purge it of its contents, but that would require him walking the three blocks to the 2-4 store. If Ruiz was working his shift down at the 2-4 store he would surely let Tommy grab a bottle off the shelf at 100% discount. If Buttmunch Artie was working, he could forget about it. What day is this, thought Tommy? Tuesday. Artie worked till six on Tuesdays. That was all beside the point, anyhow. Tommy did not want to go outside. It was his day off and he just wanted to hang out in his apartment and get high.

Tommy Balls shook his head and smiled at the television. Magnum, P.I. was being reprimanded by Higgins, the care-taker of the Robin Masters Estate, for borrowing his camera without asking. Why do I have to live in Buffalo? Why can't I be living for free in Hawaii like Magnum, thought Tommy.

"Fuckin' Higgins," said Tommy Balls.

Tommy got up and stretched his arms above his head un-til they cracked. He picked up a black, Metallica tour T-shirt from the arm of the couch, sniffed it, then pulled it over his tattooed torso. Sure enough, behind the bathroom door he found a white plastic bucket. He removed the dark sock and searched the bathroom for a good place to drape it, settling on the sink. He found a steak knife sticking out from the dirty dishes in the kitchen sink and a pair of scissors on the table under a stack of *High Times* and empty plastic CD cases. He gave a futile look inside the garbage can for a soda pop bottle. On top of the wet trash was a paperback self-help book entitled *Am I Crazy?* by Dr. Sage Mennox. Tommy Balls had received the book as a gift from his mother, a recovering sippy alcoholic and Born Again Christian. He called his mother a "sippy alcoholic" because that is what she was: a sippy here, a sippy there, all day around the house until the evening news rolled around and she was rip-roaring drunk and looking for conflict. Tommy's mother was not out the door one minute after giving him the book when he had deposited it in the shitcan. Two years ago his mother had become a loyal and devoted follower of the TV talk show mental health guru, Dr. Mennox. Some people need desperately to follow someone, thought Tommy. His mother had been off the booze since she began devouring every book written by Dr. Mennox, and, in Tommy's opinion, that was good. However, she was infinitely more annoying as a Christian than she ever was as a drunk. His mother was convinced that Dr. Mennox had saved her life. She had dog-eared dozens of pages in each of his books and could recite chapter and verse. She said Dr. Mennox had taught her how to be, how did she say it? *Mentally fit and physically strong.* He was the gatekeeper who kept her off the Road to Crazy. Tommy had seen the good doctor once on one of the daytime talk shows. He thought he seemed stiff and impersonal for a self-help guru. He did have a nice tan on his bald head, though. And his suit must have cost $3,000. He wore cufflinks, too. Tommy always paid attention to whether someone wore button-down cuffs or cufflinks. For Tommy, cufflinks were the dead giveaway that you had money.

Tommy's father wore cufflinks. He was a successful Orchard Park dentist who enjoyed hand-rolled cigars, Cutty Sark, and spending his evenings at the bar in the Knights of Columbus Hall. He spent most of his free time avoiding his family, which he often referred to as "The Great Failed Experiment." Tommy's father believed in hard work, discipline and sacrifice. He was a Navy man, enlisting at the end of the Vietnam War. He rose to the rank of Chief and, when his last enlistment ended, went to dental school nights and weekends on the GI Bill. While in school, he supported his wife and son with a factory job at Bethlehem Steel. He had recently concluded that his wife was a loon and his son Tom was the laziest sonofabitch he had ever met.

While his son was across town searching for the implements to construct a homemade bong, former Navy Chief Tom Ballisteri, Sr. was sitting on a barstool among friends and fellow veterans at the Knights of Columbus Hall on Delaware Avenue. He raised his glass of Budweiser and offered this toast to his wife and son, "Here's to the Great Failed Experiment."

Tommy Balls stood with his hands on his hips in the middle of his kitchenette. He needed a two-litre soda pop bottle but was in no mood to walk down to the 2-4 store, and even if he did, he did not want to pay for it once he got there. Maybe I can ask the fat bastard downstairs, Tommy thought. What was his name? Fred...Frank...Franklin!

"Frankie!" shouted Tommy Balls alone in his kitchenette. "Hey, Frankie," he said, offering up his best impression of a New Jersey Wise Guy. He knew Franklin could not hear him. "Hey, Frankie! You got any empty pop bottles you fat bastard!" Tommy started laughing at his own improvisational comedy invention. "Hey fat Frankie, give Uncle Tommy your empty soda pop bottles!"

He decided he would go downstairs and ask Franklin if he had any soda pop bottles. But first I will watch the rest of this episode of *Magnum, P.I.*, thought Tommy. He melted into his secondhand couch and cranked the volume on the television as loud as it could go.

"Motherfucking *Magnum, P.I.!*" screamed Tommy Balls.

CHAPTER

3

IF FRANKLIN HAD to choose whom to murder it would have been a coin toss between Mr. Allspice and his landlord, Mr. Olivetti. Even though Franklin thought they were both assholes, the quality of Franklin's life would have improved immediately if Mr. Allspice was to suddenly disappear. Mr. Olivetti was a once-a-month problem. Mr. Allspice was a miserable bastard and an everyday pain-in-the-ass. That was a moot point now though, with a dead Mr. Olivetti sprawled out on Franklin's kitchenette floor.

Franklin was fat, but not stupid. He did not want to go to jail for murdering Mr. Olivetti. He had to get rid of the body. He meditated silently on his orange chair. Disposing of the body properly is where most criminals mess up and get caught. Wow, I am a criminal now, thought Franklin. I'm a wanted man. Franklin decided it would be best to brainstorm. He removed a fresh yellow legal pad from the crisper and began a list. He thought it would be fun to play Devil's

Advocate, so beside each idea he jotted down why it might not work.

1.) Dump him in the Buffalo or Niagara River. *How can I be sure I won't be seen? The bodies always wash up eventually.*

2.) Bury him. *Where? I don't own a shovel. It's a lot of physical labour and I am not in the best of shape.*

3.) Burn him. *Again, where? Won't the smell be too noticeable? Still, though, not the worst option.*

4.) Cut him up. *Not a chance. I don't have the stomach or the proper tools.*

5.) Make it look like suicide. *Not bad. Must look convincing, though.*

6.) Car accident, ie: put him in his truck and roll him off a cliff. *What cliff? I live in the city.*

Franklin saw some potential in these ideas. Maybe a combination of two or three of them would be just the ticket. He went to his window and looked west down Garner to Dewitt and then east to Grant Street. Mr. Olivetti's tan 1994 Chevy S-10 was parked on the same side of the street, three doors down.

Summer was ending and the days were getting shorter and cooler. Franklin knew he could expect it to be dark around 8 o'clock. He looked at his watch: 6:15. Franklin leaned over and squeezed Mr. Olivetti's bare, left bicep. His skin was clammy and cold and his muscles were beginning to stiffen. It was just over eight hours since Franklin murdered his landlord. The body had to go tonight, and as far as Franklin was concerned, it could not get dark fast enough.

It occurred to Franklin that the only dead person he had ever seen up close was his mother. In her casket she looked like a wax mannequin moulded to resemble his mother, he thought. She had, as she called it, "cancer of the noggin" and died twenty-six years ago on Franklin's fifteenth birthday. Bernard was twenty-two years old and had just been accepted into graduate school at the University of Buffalo. Franklin could not ever recall seeing his mother healthy. She had no energy for playing the game of life; it seemed she decided early on that she was destined to lose it. He remembered placing a postcard depicting the Swiss Alps in her hand after the wake, before they sealed her casket forever. Those snow-tipped mountains were Franklin's vision of Heaven.

Franklin and Bernard had never known their father, not even his first name. Their mother forbade them to speak of him and they obeyed. For all Franklin knew, or cared, his father lived next door to him on Garner. It would not surprise him if his father were someone like Mr. Olivetti. Or Mr. Olivetti, himself.

My mother's death face was more serene than Mr. Olivetti's, thought Franklin. The landlord's frozen stare and garish grin unnerved Franklin. He reached down and closed Mr. Olivetti's eyes with a sweep of his hand. He reached into Mr. Olivetti's trouser pocket and pulled out the keys to his Chevy.

Franklin had decided on some plans of action. He would

wait until dark, carry Mr. Olivetti out to his truck and dump
him in the back underneath the cap. He had not yet decided
whether to roll the truck into the Niagara River with Mr.
Olivetti in the driver's seat, set the truck on fire and push it
off a cliff, or choose a third option he had not yet thought of.
He would have to wait and see what sort of mood he was in
after dark. He sat at his table, rubbing the bump on his head
and mulling his options. He noticed 101 moving around her
living room in the yellow building across the street. He
snatched his binoculars from the counter in the kitchenette
and scurried back to his perch at the window.

She was vacuuming. She was wearing a red cotton top with
short sleeves and a low neckline. Franklin followed the smooth
outline of her thin, tan legs up to her khaki shorts and delighted as her ass danced with each stroke of the vacuum. He
decided that he would have her again tonight in the bubble
bath after this Olivetti business was settled. He burned the image of her bouncing breasts into his mind for later reference.
She was talking to someone. Who was it? Aha! Beyond the top
of the couch Franklin saw her teenage daughter, Little 101. She
was watching a music video on the television with her back
to Franklin. He focused the binoculars. The volume bar graphic
appeared on the television and crept across the screen. The
mother was now yelling at her daughter. The volume bar appeared again. This time it stretched across the screen as far as
it could go. The mother seized the remote from her daughter
and turned off the television. Little 101 stood up. Franklin tried

to steady the binoculars on her blossoming breasts. It was no use. She stormed out of the living room and he jerked the binoculars from window to window. Where did she go? thought Franklin. He returned his lecherous gaze to the living room. The mother was now gone, too. The show was over. He had hoped to kill some time until dark, watching the women across the street. It was just one more thing that did not go Franklin's way that Tuesday.

Franklin unfolded a blue wool blanket and laid it over Mr. Olivetti. Later, he would need to determine the most expeditious way to get his carcass down the sidewalk. It would be a good idea to move the Chevy closer to the building, he thought.

There was a knock at the door.

Franklin froze in place. The knock came again. Five, swift thumps at his apartment door. Should I ignore it, he wondered? Was that the smart thing to do? Aw shit. He pulled the door open until it was stopped abruptly by the security chain. Outside in the foyer stood Tommy Balls. It's the pothead from upstairs, thought Franklin.

"Hey Guy! It's your upstairs neighbour, Tommy Balls," said Tommy. He noticed Franklin was wearing only his underwear.

"I see," said Franklin. Don't say too much, he cautioned himself. Speak only when spoken to.

"Er, yeah. Do you have any, like, empty soda pop bottles? The two-litre size?"

Franklin had a dozen of them below his sink. "No," he answered.

"Oh," said Tommy. "Are you sure? I only need one. Shouldn't you, like, check or something?"

Don't panic, Franklin. Stay cool. "Hold on," said Franklin. He closed the door, ran to the sink, grabbed an empty green bottle, and dashed back to the door. Tommy Balls was startled when the door opened again and he jumped backwards.

"Ginger ale OK?" asked Franklin.

"Yeah, that's fine dude," said Tommy.

Franklin attempted to pass the bottle through the space between the door and the wall. The bottle was too fat. Franklin jammed the bottle into the narrow opening and the plastic popped and crinkled.

"Whoa, dude," said Tommy. "Can't you just open the door?"

"No," said Franklin. "Pull!"

Tommy Balls did not know what to make of this corpulent recluse on the other side of the door, but with the final component to his new gravity bong just inches away, he grabbed the bottle with both hands and started pulling. Franklin pounded the bottle with his fist as it wormed through the opening. Then it reached the hard plastic base.

"It's stuck," said Tommy. "Can't you just open the frickin' door?"

"If you want the damn bottle, pull!" said Franklin.

Tommy tightened his grip, gave the bottle a violent yank, and freed it from the doorway. The effort sent him three steps backwards.

"All right then. Nice to see you," said Franklin as he closed the door.

"Wait!" yelled Tommy Balls. "Have you seen Mr. Olivetti today? He's supposed to be coming over to fix my sink. It drips."

"Oh, I killed him," said Franklin.

"Mmm," said Tommy. "Well if you see him, tell him my sink is still dripping."

"Tell him yourself," said Franklin. "He's dead on my kitchenette floor."

"Ok, dude. Just tell him about the sink."

Tommy headed up the stairs. Franklin the Funny Fat Guy, he thought. Mr. Mirth. Put some frickin' clothes on, Tubby. It's not *that* hot outside.

Franklin latched the door and banged his head against it, leaving it there to rest. I handled that badly, he thought. He wondered if that pothead upstairs knew what Mr. Olivetti's Chevy truck looked like. Franklin doubted the kid had ever looked out his window. Since the day he moved in, his view of the street had been obscured by a tie-dyed bed sheet. What the hell did he want with an empty two-litre soda pop bottle, wondered Franklin?

"You rent to some real winners," Franklin said to Mr. Olivetti.

Franklin's dog, nuzzled against the dead body, was snoring.

AFTER DARK, FRANKLIN pulled on a grey T-shirt, tan shorts and a pair of rubber-soled leather sandals. He grabbed Mr. Olivetti's keys off the table and headed outside. He closed the doors in the breezeway silently and crept down the stone steps to the sidewalk. There were no street lamps on Garner but a three-quarter moon hung in the night sky. The lunar light illuminated the car tops that lined both sides of the street. It seemed to Franklin that there were more people out in the neighbourhood on a Tuesday than he had ever seen, but he attributed that to nerves. Franklin headed east on Garner towards Mr. Olivetti's Chevy. His ears felt hot and the hairs on his neck tickled as he sensed the weight of someone's stare behind him. He glanced back over his left shoulder at the building. There in his window was the puffy red face of Mr. Allspice in 2A. That nosey, hawk-eyed sonofabitch, thought Franklin. He is going to complicate matters this evening. Franklin began walking again. He reached Mr. Olivetti's Chevy truck and was sure Mr. Allspice could not see him anymore, but he kept walking anyway. Franklin knew the old buzzard liked to take a stroll out onto the front porch whenever he suspected something foul was afoot in the neighbourhood. Franklin walked and thought. He tried to focus all his mental energy on removing the body in his kitchenette. He was still not certain which course of action was best. One thing was absolutely certain; he had to dispose of the body that night. A new day would bring new problems. And when it did, he did not want Mr. Olivetti still lying in the middle of his kitchenette. Franklin reached the end of Garner. He decided to continue north up Grant Street all the way to the Open 2-4 store. He thought a 40-ounce bottle of Old English and a Mars Bar would help settle his nerves.

Three-foot high red neon letters illuminated the corner of Grant Street and Forest Avenue. "We Never Close" was the sign above the Open 2-4 store. Franklin pulled the door and it was locked. They were closed. The lights in the store were on, but no one was behind the counter. There was a handwritten note taped on the glass door from the inside:

"Our freezer's busted. Sorry for the temporary inconvenience."

He cupped his hands and pressed his greasy nose against the glass to investigate the store's interior. Not a soul to be found. Shouldn't there be someone in there with a mop? What the hell were they doing in there, he wondered?

"Probably smoking dope in the stockroom," said a female voice from behind Franklin. He turned. It was the pretty teenage daughter from the yellow building across the street— Little 101. "I know you," she said. "You're the man who lives across the street from me."

"Do they do that?" asked Franklin. "Do they smoke pot in the stockroom?" He tried not to stare at her budding breasts beneath her white cotton tank top. Could she see the lust in his eyes?

"Oh yeah," she said. "They smoke back there all the time. I've been back there with them a few times. Mostly college guys, some older. They're pretty cool. The weed is bitchin'."

Franklin did not know how to respond to that.

"I'm going home right now. Do you want to walk with me?" she asked.

"Sure. Of course. Er, yes," said Franklin. They walked side-by-side for half a block without speaking before the girl said something that almost made Franklin lose his bowels.

"My friend and I call you Mr. Peepers," she said.

Franklin's heart stopped beating and his sphincter pinched tight as he waited for the other shoe to drop.

"I know you watch me and my mom. It's OK, my mom doesn't know. I see you over there in your window with your specs behind the big maple tree. I don't mind. In fact, I sort of like it. How old are you, fifty?"

"Forty-one."

"When my friend and I are old enough we're going to be dancers in Canada. I'll bet you never heard anyone say that before. We'll get to wear sexy clothes, and we'll own hundreds of awesome shoes, and we'll be able to do whatever we want because we'll be making tons and tons of cash. We're even going to start our own website. My friend Suzy and I have it all planned out."

Franklin would definitely log on to that, he thought. But first he would need a computer—and a phone. He could not decide whether he was thrilled by, or terrified of, the young girl. He resolved that he was both. He felt wonderfully nauseous and had, for the moment, forgotten all about Mr. Olivetti.

"Sex is about control, don't you think?" she asked, arching one of her thin, brown eyebrows towards Franklin. "I don't let you see any more than I want you to. I have the control. It's the same with the boys at the 2-4 store. I don't show them, or give them, any more than I want to. That's the way it should be. Don't you think?"

"Mmm," nodded Franklin eagerly.

As they turned west onto Garner, Franklin's new friend ran three strides ahead and turned around. "You have sad eyes," said the girl. "But sort of an impish smile. You probably wouldn't be bad looking if you lost some weight. I'm not saying that to hurt your feelings or anything. You just really should lose some weight. Being fat is unhealthy. How tall are you?"

Before he could answer she was back-to-back with him. She placed her hand flat between their heads and turned around. "Wow. I'm almost an inch taller than you."

"My brother Bernard is 6'3"," said Franklin.

"I guess you got the short end of the stick, huh?" she said. "He should have given some to you." She ran ahead and turned around again. "What are you doing tonight at midnight, Mr. Peepers? I think that tonight I'll give you a show you'll never forget." She leaned forward, cupped her young breasts and gave them a provocative squeeze. Then she delivered a pouty kiss into the night air and took off running towards her yellow building. "Don't forget your specs tonight, Mr. Peepers!" she called over her shoulder as she ran up Garner, up her stairs and into her building.

Franklin wiped the sweat off his forehead with the sleeve of his t-shirt. He was so thirsty he could barely swallow. He looked at his watch: 9:05. Whatever he was going to do with Mr. Olivetti, he positively had to be finished by midnight. He walked up to Mr. Olivetti's Chevy pickup and looked in through the passenger-side window. "Sonofabitch," Franklin said. The Chevy was a standard transmission and Franklin had never learned how to drive a stick.

FRANKLIN THREW MR. OLIVETTI'S keys down on the table. Mr. Allspice's light was off when he came in. That was a good sign. I'm not surprised he's in bed by nine o'clock, Franklin thought. The crabby bastard is up by five every morning. He grabbed a can of Moxie cola from the refrigerator and took a long swallow. He sat down in his orange chair and looked across the street at Little 101's window. The blinds were down and the curtains were drawn. I never asked her what her name was. Probably better that way, he thought. He was percolating with nervous energy. He rubbed the tender bump on his head and took three, long gulps of soda pop, finishing the can. Franklin got back up again and removed the ice tray from the freezer. He twisted the tray until the ice cracked then spilled the contents into a plastic grocery bag. He twisted the bag tightly around the ice, sat back in his chair at the window, and placed the bag atop the bump on his head.

Franklin closed his eyes and replayed his conversation with Little 101. This is what Switzerland would be like, he thought. It would be this feeling every moment of every day. He wanted to blow his alphorn but the timing was imprudent.

"I have to get up off my fetid, fat ass and get rid of Mr. Olivetti if I want to be back in this orange chair by midnight," Franklin said conspiratorially to his sleeping hound dog.

CHAPTER

4

T OMMY BALLS SAT at the edge of his faded, corduroy
couch and inventoried the objects laid out on his coffee
table: one white, plastic bucket; one serrated knife; one pair
of scissors; one empty, slightly crushed, two-litre plastic
soda pop bottle; one dime bag of Bobo's Nicaraguan weed;
and a cocktail napkin with a diagram of Tony's gravity bong.

It was 8:50 and the *Magnum, P.I.* marathon was winding
down to its last three episodes. Tommy decided he had pro-
crastinated long enough. It was time to build the bong.

First Tommy decided to select the proper music for bong building. He laid the nylon, zippered case containing his collection
of 160 CDs across his lap and began thumbing through the pages.
Metallica, "Enter Sandman": mmm, no. Jimi Hendrix, "Purple
Haze": getting warmer. "Riders on the Storm" by The Doors:
almost there. Aha! Perfect. James Brown, "I Feel Good."
Tommy slid the CD out of its plastic sleeve and placed it in the
player. Now for the task at hand, he thought.

He filled the white bucket halfway with water from the bathtub. Next, he poked the knife through the soda pop bottle just above the hard plastic base and sawed it up and down a few times to get the cut-line started. He used the scissors to make a clean cut all the way around the bottle with the plastic base as a guideline. Tommy removed the white plastic screw cap and discarded it over his shoulder.

"I'll leave that for the cleaning lady," Tommy said.

He set the plastic bucket of water between his legs then packed a monster bowl of Nicaraguan weed and sparked it. He placed the bottomless soda pop bottle in the water inside the bucket. Tommy took a long drag off the pipe, bent over, and blew it into the mouth of the soda bottle then capped it with his thumb. The bottle was sitting in the water as far down as it could go. He marveled at how a cloud of the sweet smoke formed above the cold water.

"I *feeel* nice. Sugar and spice," sang Tommy.

Tommy looked up at the television and smiled in anticipation of a glorious hit. Magnum and his friend, TC, were in a helicopter somewhere high above the lush, volcanic mountaintops of Hawaii.

Tommy bent down, uncorked his thumb from the bottleneck and covered it with his mouth. He sucked the sweet smoke deep into his lungs as he slowly raised the soda pop bottle out of the water. He got halfway up through the water, then erupted into a coughing fit, spraying saliva and marijuana fog all over his coffee table. He flopped back into the old couch, still coughing sporadically, all smiles. His eyes looked like they had been rinsed in chlorine then replaced in their sockets. That was the best hit of my life, Tommy decided. Kudos to Tony, the would-be hotel manager. His gravity bong was a complete success.

"Fucking gravity bong, baby!" exalted Tommy to the four bare walls of his apartment.

CHAPTER

5

FRANKLIN HAD TO use his own car to move Mr. Olivetti's body and that was all there was to it. He had no idea how he was going to remove Mr. Olivetti's Chevy from Garner Street, but he thought it best to worry about one thing at a time. What he did know was this: He had to do something, anything, with his fat, dead, Italian landlord before midnight.

Then, like a thunderclap, the solution was clear. He could take Mr. Olivetti back to his own house in Lackawanna, a rural suburb of Buffalo. He lived alone, a widower, and he had a barn behind his house that he used as a workshop. Franklin had been there twice in his four years as a tenant at 100 Garner. The first time was to sign his rental agreement. The second time was to pick up the simulated-wood table that he was now leaning on, plotting the removal of Mr. Olivetti's murdered corpse. Lackawanna was about twenty minutes south. If all went to plan, he would be back at the window, binoculars in hand, with time to spare. What worried him were the dark, country roads. Franklin did not much care for driving to begin with, but he despised driving in the dark. I'll just have to gut it out, he thought. I'll take this dead bastard out to his house and I will deal with his truck when I get back.

Franklin stepped out onto the porch. The breeze was cool. He looked west to Dewitt and east to Grant Street. No one was out on the sidewalks or in the street. Music was blasting from behind Tommy Balls' window. Franklin recognized it and began to sing softly, "I *feeeeel* good. You knew that I would."

He could see that the apartment light was on behind Tommy's tie-dyed tapestry. Franklin knew Miss Parson from Grover Cleveland Elementary would be disappointed, but he was willing to assume that Tommy Balls was either sky high or passed out cold. He was right on both counts.

Franklin groaned as he allowed gravity to suck his buttocks into the concave driver's seat of his silver 1986 Pontiac T1000 hatchback. He settled in with a flurry of weight shifts and instrument adjustments, then pulled the Pontiac up to the end of the sidewalk in front of 100 Garner. Unless he could find a better solution he would have to drag Mr. Olivetti all the way from the front porch and hope for the best. Franklin groaned again as he lurched forward out of the Pontiac, leaving it rocking on its four bald tires.

FRANKLIN SPOTTED A RED Radio Flyer wagon. He knew it belonged to the strawberry-haired kid next door with the giant melon on his shoulders who always wore the same dirty green T-shirt. The metal wagon was in the neighbour's yard, just inside the picket fence. Franklin reached over the fence and snatched the wagon. He leaned it on the other side of the stone steps, out of sight, and went into the building.

Mr. Olivetti was about an inch shorter than Franklin and not one chocolate chip cookie less than 220 pounds. Franklin rolled the body onto a green army blanket, then re-covered it with the blue wool blanket. He grabbed two corners of the wool blanket at Mr. Olivetti's feet and pulled the body across the cracked linoleum floor to the door. Franklin maneuvered the body around the door as he opened it into his apartment. Out in the foyer, he dragged him the six feet across the hardwood floor to the inside door of the breezeway. He reached into the breezeway and clicked off the porch light. The inside door was spring activated and had to be worked around the body every few inches as it kept trying to close. Franklin felt the strain in his back and groaned as he slid the body six more feet across the checkerboard tile of the breezeway to the outside door. The inside door, which was being held open by Mr. Olivetti's smiling head, slammed shut when he pulled the body all the way into the breezeway.

Franklin froze. He listened. He waited. He could feel his pulse pounding in his ears. Nothing happened.

Franklin knew that if Mr. Allspice were to materialize from behind his apartment door, the jig most definitely would be up. He worked the outside door around Mr. Olivetti's stiff elbow and pulled him onto the porch. Franklin, hands on knees, was panting. Five stone steps and twenty feet of sidewalk separated Mr. Olivetti and the trunk of Franklin's Pontiac T1000. Franklin could not recall when he had been so winded. Good golly, thought Franklin, I'm having a hell of a time moving this fat bastard.

From the sidewalk behind him Franklin heard the jingle of a dog's collar. He could not bear to turn around but he looked anyhow. Across the street was a young man he did not recognize wearing a leather jacket with chains jangling around the shoulders, walking his Rottweiler. The dog walker was looking right at him but Franklin had no idea what he was able to see. He and Franklin locked eyes for an instant. Franklin nodded like a good neighbour. The dog, sniffing the ground and pulling the leash, tugged the dog walker forward a few steps. He turned the corner and headed north up Dewitt.

Thank god nobody in this city gives a good goddamn what you're up to anymore, he thought. Hey buddy, I have my dead landlord here wrapped in blankets. Want to have a looky-loo?

The dog walker gave Franklin a powerful surge of adrenaline. He pulled the body to the edge of the porch and let Mr. Olivetti's feet dangle over the first stone step. Franklin grabbed the red Radio Flyer wagon and placed it at the base of the steps. He pulled Mr. Olivetti by the feet down the steps (bumpity-bump) and hoisted him face up onto the wagon. Franklin went around to the front of the wagon and began to pull it towards the street by the handle. The hard, plastic wheels ground against the cement and created an awful racket. (This was a bad idea. Bad idea.) Franklin started running backwards, pulling the wagon with both hands clenched firmly around the handle. Suddenly he heard the creak of flimsy metal and the arm and handle of the wagon snapped off in his hands.

Franklin let out a girlish shriek and whipped the broken handle into the neighbour's shrubs.

He dashed to the rear of the wagon, grabbed two fistfuls of Mr. Olivetti's flabby thighs, and started to run on the balls of his feet towards the Pontiac's open trunk. The hard plastic tires roared against the pavement. The end of the sidewalk was not flush and the front tires slammed against the lip, sending Mr. Olivetti sailing ass over teakettle. Franklin found himself snarled in the green army blanket and shrieked again as he spun 360 degrees to see if anyone was witness to this morbid burlesque.

Mr. Olivetti was on his back, smiling. Franklin squatted beside him (keep your back straight, lift with your legs) and slowly lifted Mr. Olivetti like a wounded dog.

"Oof," groaned Franklin as he rose to his feet. He waddled over the curb and deposited the body into the trunk, nearly falling in with it.

Franklin slammed the trunk shut and the porch light popped on. He wheeled around in terror to see Mr. Allspice standing inside the breezeway in his blue-striped flannel pyjamas. Mr. Allspice stepped out onto the porch.

"Why was the porch light off?"

"Um (pant), I (pant), uh (pant)," Franklin struggled to catch his breath. His clothes were soaked in sweat. "I think it's busted."

"It's not busted, you fool," said Mr. Allspice. "All I did was turn it on."

"Oh. Good job then," said Franklin. "I think you fixed it."

Mr. Allspice moved another stride closer to the stone steps. "What is all the commotion out here?" asked Mr. Allspice.

"I'm packing."

"Packing?" said Mr. Allspice. "At this hour? Are you leaving on a trip?"

"I'm moving," said Franklin. "I'm moving to, um... Switzerland."

"Oh, well that is good news," said Mr. Allspice. "Let the Swiss deal with you and your ridiculous horn. Good riddance, I say. If I weren't so old, I would help you pack. Maybe this time Mr. Olivetti can bring in a suitable tenant." Mr. Allspice turned and walked back through the breezeway. "I'm sure you'll love their chocolates, you fat twit. Keep this light on!" The inside door slammed shut.

Hot dog, thought Franklin. The goomba is in the trunk. Speaking of hot dogs, I haven't eaten all day. He looked at his watch, two minutes 'til ten.

THE DRIVE DOWN to Lackawanna was not as treacherous as Franklin had feared. There were only a few turns after he turned off Rte. 5 and there was barely another car on the road. He remembered the turn-off from the main drag and started down a gloomy, meandering country road. He drove for about five miles and began to look for a white picket fence on the right-hand side. After the fence it was two, maybe three mailboxes. Franklin remembered Mr. Olivetti's mailbox had a red reflector screwed to it. Despite the bright moon, the road was black and seemed to pitch into a 45-degree turn every hundred yards. Twice Franklin shrieked as deer materialized on the side of the road, their eyes shimmering in the headlights like tiny mirrors. Mr. Olivetti was beginning to get a little ripe in the back. The Pontiac T1000 was a fine machine, but it was also a hatchback. So even though technically the dead body was in the trunk, only the back seat separated Franklin's olfactory system from Mr. Olivetti's carcass. Franklin turned on the interior light and looked at his watch, 10:24. Mr. Olivetti had been dead for almost eleven hours. He rolled down the window.

Franklin recognized the white picket fence and turned down the radio. He wondered why people always do that, turn down the radio as they near their destination.

Three mailboxes later he spied the red reflector and turned right onto the long gravel driveway. He did not think it was possible, but the driveway was darker and gloomier than the road. All these damn trees, he thought. The headlights rolled across Mr. Olivetti's white clapboard house as Franklin followed the driveway back to the barn. He executed a perfect three-point turn, backed the car up to the barn door and killed the engine. Franklin extricated himself from the Pontiac and stepped out onto the gravel driveway. The tiny stones crunched under his rubber sandals. The crickets sounded like they were ten feet tall and closing in on him. The woods were alive with a thousand pairs of eyes. He popped the trunk, looked down at Mr. Olivetti's twisted corpse and was struck in sharp clarity with the criminal thing he was about to do. He turned away from the trunk and vomited his Moxie cola onto the driveway. There wasn't much to it since he had not eaten all day, mostly foam. He smoothed gravel over it and stamped it down with his sandal. Franklin walked around in a little circle trying to get his bearings.

"Okey dokey," he said. "How do you want to die the second time, Albert? How about death by…cigarette? It's a hell of a lot more dignified than the way you died this morning."

He opened the barn door, pulled a rubber ball dangling from a string in the workshop and a bulb popped on. Franklin pulled the blankets off Mr. Olivetti and lifted him out of the trunk. He laid him on the blue blanket, dragged him into the barn and propped him up against the worktable.

"I'll be right back," said Franklin. "Don't you go anywhere."

Franklin used Mr. Olivetti's keys to get in through the back door. He stepped into the kitchen and immediately recognized the lingering stench of Parmesan cheese. He ripped off a paper towel from above the sink and used it to start pulling open drawers, looking for a box of kitchen matches.

He threw open several cupboards and found a half carton of Salems. Franklin removed a pack and put it in the pocket of his T-shirt. No matches in the kitchen, so Franklin walked into the living room. There were dozens of framed photographs nailed to the brown paneling. In a homemade wooden rack above the television Mr. Olivetti had a collection of two dozen chrome Zippo lighters. The lighters had all sorts of designs and phrases painted on them: a colourful, bald eagle, an American flag, the *Playboy* bunny logo, the insignia of the U.S. Navy. Franklin selected one that had the Chevy symbol painted on it.

He put the lighter in his shirt pocket and used the paper towel to rearrange the others so it did not look like one was missing.

He wanted to poke around the house a bit more. He knew this would be his only opportunity. Part of it was curiosity, but it was also an unfamiliar sense of power. He knew that at that moment he could take anything he wanted from Mr. Olivetti's house.

On top of the television set were several photographs. Mr. and Mrs. Olivetti's black and white wedding portrait was the largest. The pose showed them from the chest up, smiling at some far-off point of interest. There were also colour photos of Mr. Olivetti's daughter with her husband and two daughters.

Franklin stared into the eyes of Mr. Olivetti's daughter. He focused on the red dots inside her pupils as she smiled over her shoulder in front of a Christmas tree.

"Your father was a bad man," said Franklin. "He was worse than you'll ever know. I'm sorry I killed him, but I'm not sorry he's dead."

Franklin checked the time: 10:54. No time for this, he thought. I have to get this show on the road.

FRANKLIN PULLED DOWN a can of turpentine from Mr. Olivetti's supply shelf. He read the side of the can, WARNING: FLAMMABLE. Let's hope so, he thought. He soaked a rag in the turpentine, rubbed it onto Mr. Olivetti's shirtsleeves, then poured some onto the worktable. The liquid flowed quickly across the table, spilling off onto an oilcloth draping a bale of hay Mr. Olivetti used as a chair. Franklin shook the remaining contents of the can onto the walls like a bishop distributing holy water.

He dropped the rag on the table in front of the body. For good measure, he placed a hammer in Mr. Olivetti's cold, right hand.

"Whatcha working on, Albert?" asked Franklin. "Don't forget that you have to fix the drip on that pothead Tommy Balls' kitchen sink. You'll need a plumber's wrench for that Al, not a hammer."

Franklin lit a cigarette with the Zippo, touched it to Mr. Olivetti's lips, then dropped it onto the rag. The cloth ignited instantly. The flames simultaneously advanced up Mr. Olivetti's shirtsleeves and rolled across the worktable. The fire leapt onto the oilcloth and began to incinerate the hay bale. Franklin trundled over and held the Zippo's blue flame to the wall until a fire fluttered to life and orange and yellow waves danced seductively atop the plywood.

In seconds the fire had begun to consume the body. Mr. Olivetti's smiling face grew darker behind an orange veil of fire.

Good golly. This is the real thing, thought Franklin.

The smell of burning flesh was almost too much for him to bear, but he forced himself to watch long enough to be sure the fire was raging. He wiped the Zippo clean with his T-shirt and dropped it in the dirt at Mr. Olivetti's feet.

By the time he reached the end of the gravel driveway the fire had spread to the barn's supports and crossbeams. By the time he reached the Lackawanna town line, the structure was totally engulfed in flames and fire departments from three towns were on their way to the scene.

CHAPTER

6

LACKAWANNA FIRE INVESTIGATOR Burt Walnut was asleep next to his wife, June, when the phone rang. It was a quarter to midnight and the voice on the other end of the telephone was Lackawanna Fire Chief Billy Browski.

"How's about it, Burt? I'm sorry if I woke ya. We got a crispy critter here at a barn fire off Old Post Road. Italian fella named Olivetti. You know him?"

"Nope. Can't say as I do."

"Uh huh." Billy was calling on his cellular phone from the scene and his voice was drifting in and out. "Looks a little fishy here, Burt. We got the fire out, but you're gonna wanna look at the scene tonight before the boys get to clearing this shit and debris."

"Uh huh," said Burt Walnut.

"What's that you said, Burt? This goddamn cellular phone."

"What's the number out there?" asked Burt.

"It's 340 Old Post," said Billy. "You won't be able to miss it.

We got pumpers from three districts out here, though I imagine they'll be gone before you can get here."

"I'll be along. Don't touch nothing you don't have to," said Burt.

"How about my pecker?"

"I don't suppose anybody can stop you from touching that, Billy. It's a wonder you ain't blind."

"Ha, ha. All right Burt. Tell June I'm sorry if I woke ya's. We'll be seeing ya shortly."

June rolled towards Burt with her eyes still closed tight. She had the calm disposition of a veteran fireman's wife. She knew a call in the middle of the night was more likely work than tragedy, although Burt's job was a marriage of the two.

"What is it?" asked June into her pillow.

"Barn fire off Old Post Road. You know any Olivettis?"

"I know a Mandretti," said June.

"Nope. This one here is Olivetti and he's dead."

CHAPTER

7

FRANKLIN KNEW HE had worked his way into a hell of a fix. Part of his problem was solved, but he still had to figure out what to do with Mr. Olivetti's Chevy pickup truck. Why didn't Bernard teach me how to drive a stick shift? he lamented. It would have been a much better plan if the truck were out at the house. Now he could be sure that the police would come looking for it. Well, what's done is done, he thought. Besides, if I drove him out there in his truck, how would I have gotten home? He needed a plan for the Chevy, but he couldn't think straight. All he cared about was that it was ten minutes till midnight and he would be sitting at his window with his binoculars in just a few moments.

He drove slowly past Mr. Olivetti's Chevy and parked on the opposite side of the street. I'll worry about that damned thing after, he thought.

Franklin could not suppress his anticipation. What would

Little 101 do? How much would she show? How far would she go? He had no idea what to expect. His pants were ready to explode. He broke into a fat man's run across the street all the way into 100 Garner. He threw his keys onto the table, left the lights off and pulled his orange chair up to the window with his binoculars in hand. Her window was black. The blinds were down and the curtains were drawn. Franklin checked his watch: 11:56. He fingered the knot on his head. I should probably put some more ice on that, he thought. His dog started licking the salty sweat from his leg.

"Knock it off," hissed Franklin. "Go get a drink of water."

Her bedroom light popped on. A dark shadow passed behind the shades and they began to slowly rise. He placed his elbows on the windowsill and then pressed the binoculars against his eye sockets until they ached. From behind her silky curtains he saw her. She was swaying back and forth, moving to some silent rhythm. He was pitching a Big Top in his pants. I may not make it to the bubble bath tonight, he thought. A second silhouette stepped into the window frame. The mother? thought Franklin. No, not the mother. It was another girl, another teenager. Maybe the friend—what was her name—Suzy! The two girls were hugging and dancing, running their hands slowly up and down each other's backs. This is better than I imagined it would be, thought Franklin. Good golly, I can barely stand it!

Both girls moved out of the window frame. The curtains opened slowly as they danced back into view. Franklin could now see what they were wearing: white cotton tank tops and plaid men's boxer shorts. They danced side-by-side with their backs toward him, arms akimbo. Their hips swayed playfully, bumping their young buttocks against each other. He could see they were giggling and talking with one another. Then they stopped dancing, grabbed their waistbands, pulled down their shorts, and sat their bare rears on the windowsill. They were mooning him. But there was more. There was something written on their butts. There was a black letter drawn on each perfect cheek. Franklin nearly dropped the binoculars out onto the porch as he frantically focussed to read what was written on their butt cheeks. P...E...R...U, Peru? No, not U, V. P-E-R-V. Perv! They had spelled out "Perv" to him on their consummate, teenage asses.

The two girls, convulsed in laughter, pulled up their shorts. Then Little 101's room returned to darkness.

Franklin slumped back in his chair and let the binoculars fall to his lap. He looked at his watch. The whole show had lasted four minutes. One moment you're on top of the world, the next you're in the shitter. It was like having a woman point at your penis and laugh, he thought. As it happens, he knew how that felt, too.

Franklin grabbed Mr. Olivetti's keys off the table and stepped out onto the porch. He had no choice but to figure out how to drive a standard shift well enough to get the truck far enough away to avoid suspicion.

Franklin stormed out into the street, looked east on Garner, blinked his eyes, then released a yelp of raw elation. He broke into another fat man's run. There was no mistaking it—the shattered glass. There was no explaining it—the vacant space. Someone had stolen Mr. Olivetti's tan 1994 Chevy S-10 pickup truck while he was being humiliated by two wicked, lovely teenage strumpets. Some marvelous, wonderful, beautiful, punk-ass sonofabitch. God bless this crummy city, he thought. "God bless Buffalo, New York!" screamed Franklin into the midnight sky.

"Shut your hole, fatso!" called back one of Franklin's neighbours.

CHAPTER

8

BURT WALNUT CROUCHED in the wet grass and soot along the outside perimeter of what used to be Albert Olivetti's tool barn. He picked up bits of dirt and charred wood, studied them, smelled them, and, for the most part, put them back down. Burt was wearing a navy blue windbreaker with the letters LFD emblazoned on the back in white. He was wearing a red tartan flannel shirt over a white T-shirt, blue jeans, Wolverine work boots and a red, white and blue Buffalo Bills cap. He made his way around the scene with his eyes fixed on the ground, kicking soot and debris, and bending down when it seemed pertinent.

Billy Browski had changed out of his fireproof coat and pants and replaced his helmet with a well-worn LFD baseball cap. "What d'ya make of it, Burt?"

"Don't look like arson from the outside," said Burt Walnut.

"How about from the inside?"

"Hmm," said Burt.

"We found this Zippo lighter in the dirt not three feet from the body. Could be he sparked something he was working with, fuel or paint thinner maybe. Could be he was just smoking where he shouldn't have been." Billy tossed the plastic Baggie holding the soot-covered lighter into Burt's hands.

"Hmm," said Burt.

"I for one can't figure out what this fella was supposed to be working on out here," said Billy. "Not just because of the late hour, that's not so unusual when you've got no wife telling you it's time to come in. You know what I'm saying there, Burt. But we found a rubber grip hammer melted to this fella's skin and bone and I don't know what the hell he was out here hammering. There was nothing laying around the body or the worktable that needed hammerin'. Unless it was wood. And any fool knows that you use a mallet with wood. Judging from these tools, this fella's no beginner carpenter."

"What are the police saying?" asked Burt. "What does Fred say?"

"You know Fred. Mum's the word until the autopsy is performed. He's calling it an 'open investigation'."

"Mmm-hmm," said Burt. "I got two questions right off the bat. One is, if this fella started the fire himself, by accident say, why didn't he run out of the barn? Even if he spilled gasoline all over himself from head to toe, and was getting burned up in the most hopeless sort of manner, the man would run around like a chicken trying to put out the flames. This fella here, he just burns himself up and drops right in front of his worktable. He's even still got the hammer in his hand. Unless this fella was part lemming, I've never known anybody to give up that easy."

"Can't argue there," said Billy.

"The second question is, where's this fella's vehicle?"

"Fred says he's got two vehicles registered to him. He's got a 1987 Lincoln Continental, which as you saw is under a few hundred pounds of lumber in that barn stall over there. And he's got a 1994 Chevy S-10 pickup."

"Well there ain't no engine in that Continental," said Burt. "So unless he was pushing that around town, he's been driving the Chevy."

"Well there's no sign of the Chevy truck on the property," said Billy.

"Mmm," said Burt. "Well there ain't nothing right about that."

Erie County Sheriff Fred McNally finished talking with one of his deputies and walked over to where Burt Walnut and Billy Browski were standing. The three men had known each other for more than forty years. They were hometown boys. They grew up playing the same sports and competing for the same girlfriends. Fred removed his tan cowboy hat and scratched his short, salt and pepper hair.

"This fella's got a daughter lives in Phoenix," said Fred. "I've got to head back to the office and call her."

"Billy said this fella's got a Chevy truck still unaccounted for," said Burt.

"That's right. I put out an APB on it," said Fred.

"You mind if I sniff around the house?" asked Burt.

"There weren't no fire in there," said Fred, smiling. "Not unless he was baking cookies while he was out in the barn. No, I don't mind. I got a couple deputies going through there right now. What's your take on this barn fire, Burt?"

"A lot of things don't add up. It don't strike me at first glance as accidental."

"Maybe this fella was just crazy," offered Billy. "Like that bald fella is always saying on the TV talk shows. His mind was *unfettered* and *uncooked*. What's that guy's name?"

"Mennox," said Fred. "My wife reads all his books. She says I need to stay mentally strong, or some such. She says this job of mine is leading me down the Road to Crazy. Nights like these I think she's right. Well, we'll know more about how this fella died when Bob is done with the autopsy report. I've got to go call this daughter in Phoenix. Give my best to the wives."

"Will do," said Billy.

"G'night, Fred," said Burt Walnut.

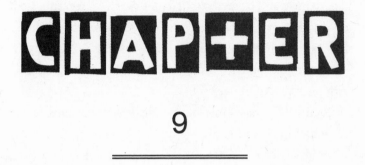

9

TOMMY BALLS WAS passed out cold on his corduroy couch when his mother knocked on his door at 10 o'clock Wednesday morning. He had passed out during the first five minutes of the last episode of the *Magnum, P.I.* marathon.

"Thomas," called Tommy's mother between knocks. "Open the door. It's your mother."

"Fuuuuck," moaned Tommy Balls. "Hold on, dude."

"Open the door. It's not right to leave your mother standing in the hallway."

Tommy swept the remaining weed on the coffee table into a Ziploc Baggie and stuck it in his back pocket. He dumped out the water from the gravity bong and left the bucket and the soda bottle in the bathtub. He gave his apartment a quick inspection: filthy. Reluctantly, he opened the door.

Tommy's mother was forty-nine years old and petite, with

a sharp nose and frosted auburn hair. She was wearing a cotton floral print church dress and white gloves. In her hands she carried a bible, a hardcover copy of *Am I Crazy* by Dr. Sage Mennox, and a white wickerwork handbag adorned with pink plastic flowers.

"Really, Thomas. How can you leave me standing in that filthy hallway? And I am not a 'dude', I am your mother."

Tommy Balls moaned and rubbed his red, puffy eye sockets.

"Your apartment is a sty, per usual, but I am not here to quarrel over that this morning." She straightened herself up as tall as her 5'3" frame would allow. "Thomas, come to church with me today."

"It's Wednesday."

"Yes, Thomas. There are services on Wednesday. The Lord is available seven days a week, not just on Sundays." Tommy's mother opened her Dr. Mennox book to the first flyleaf and read aloud: "Those who ignore their faith ignore their responsibilities, for faith is the first responsibility."

"Even if I wanted to, on principle alone, I would not go to a church that had services on Wednesdays. Besides, I have to work today."

Tommy's mother walked her fingertips over the dog-eared corners of her Dr. Mennox book and cracked it open: "Work has its purpose and its rewards, but should never serve as an escape from your problems."

"Mom! Can it with that Dr. Mennox crap. That guy is such a quack."

Tommy's mother's eyes began to well up with tears. He could sense the shit storm coming.

"I'm not going to just write you off, Thomas, I am your mother. Are you hoping that I will just ignore your drug addiction? Hmm? Are you hoping I will just pretend that everything is hunky-dory? Well, I will not. I have eyes, Thomas. I see what is happening to you. What sort of life are you making for yourself? You are well on your way down the Road To Crazy. I will not stand idly by while you punch your ticket to eternal damnation!"

"Mom. Mom, don't cry. Aw, Je-sus . . ."

"Taking the Lord's name in vain. Right in front of your Christian mother!" Tommy's mother sobbed as she crossed the room to dispose of her wet Kleenex. "And here is the thanks I get for trying," she said as she lifted the paperback copy of *Am I Crazy*, by Dr. Sage Mennox, out of the wastebasket. "If I didn't know better I would think you threw away this book because you can't read. But the truth hurts even more."

"What's the truth, mom?"

"The truth, Thomas, is that you threw away this book to break your mother's heart. Well, let me tell you something Thomas Jerome, I am not crazy. I am mentally fit and physically strong. But you, you are crazy. You walk with the heathens! Your mind is unbalanced, unfocused and impure! You have the power to change your life, Thomas, if you would only try. If you would only read Dr. Mennox." Again, Tommy's mother thumbed frantically through the worn pages. "Listen: The decision to change starts with you. But you must be willing to accept help from others. If someone who loves you offers their hand, take it. Take their hand and let them lead you off the Road to Crazy."

"Mom . . ."

"You hear that? The decision is yours, Thomas."

"Mom..."

"Come to church with me, Thomas. I beg you. Take my hand and I will lead you. Services start at 11:00. We can get a bagel and coffee on the way. Go take a shower while I iron a shirt for you."

"I have to work at noon."

Tommy's mother buried her chin into her chest and sighed. "If you feel the Lord's work is less important today than the work of the Open 24 Hours white trash convenience store, I don't know what else I can say to convince you. I know you have to earn money to pay for your hashish or grass or whatever it is you put up your nose." Tommy's mother smoothed her cotton dress with her white-gloved hands. "Your father wished to be remembered to you."

"I remember," said Tommy. "Where's he this morning? Pulling teeth or drinking scotch down at the K of C?"

"I should be going."

"Mom?"

"Yes, Thomas?" Tommy's mother crossed her arms around her books and squeezed them to her chest tightly.

"Can I borrow twenty?"

Suddenly a low, hollow tone began emanating from the floorboards. At first it sounded as though the plumbing was groaning and preparing to burst. But the volume grew louder and the pitch grew higher and Tommy's mother braced herself against the door.

"Sakes alive!" gasped Tommy's mother. "What on earth is that insane racket and where is it coming from?"

"That's the fat hermit downstairs blowing his Alpine horn," said Tommy. "Now, how about that twenty bucks?"

CHAPTER

10

FRANKLIN WAS IN a good mood Wednesday morning and he didn't care who knew it. He was blowing his alphorn and daydreaming of Swiss landscapes and majestic condors while his dog howled. He would not have cared if Mr. Allspice was home, but he knew that he was not. He had watched him leave at 8:30 that morning. That crabby bastard was probably up ten times during the night checking on the porch light, thought Franklin.

He set down his horn and went out into the breezeway to check his mail. In the street he watched a tiny lady in a flowered dress step into a blue Ford Taurus and speed away. He also noticed a little boy in a green T-shirt, strawberry hair atop his giant head, choking back tears as he plucked the mangled handle of his red wagon out of the shrubs. Franklin grabbed his mail, and Mr. Allspice's *Buffalo News,* and strolled whistling back into his apartment.

On the front page sidebar was a teaser that read: *Lackawanna Fire Kills One, see B1.* Franklin opened the paper to the Local Section. There on page one above the fold was a colour photograph of the decimated barn. The headline above it read: *Three-Alarm Fire In Lackawanna Kills One.* He scanned the article.

Lackawanna – A late night barn fire Tuesday blazed into the early morning hours, claiming the life of one man in this suburb south of Buffalo. Fire departments from three local townships responded to the blaze at 340 Old Post Road that investigators have ruled as "suspicious"...

Albert Olivetti, 63, originally of Smithtown, Long Island, suffered fatal third-degree burns . . .

"Right now we are not certain of the circumstances," said Erie County Sheriff Fred McNally. "All I can say is that it is an open investigation . . ."

Erie County Coroner Robert Fields . . . autopsy results . . .

Mr. Olivetti is survived by a daughter, Anna Bella Burton, of Phoenix, AZ and two granddaughters . . .

Franklin did not like what he was reading: "ruled suspicious," "open investigation," "autopsy results." He flopped down onto his orange chair and tried to reason it out. Of course it's suspicious, he thought. All fires are suspicious before they are ruled accidental. If it's suspicious, then it has to be an open investigation. Besides, the truck is missing and they have to find that before they can wrap things up.

Neither of those problems lead back to me. And as far as the autopsy, I watched that guy burn to a crisp with my own eyes.

Franklin thumbed through his mail and realized he had a new problem to deal with, a serious one. Today was Wednesday and there was no letter from Bernard. His brother had not missed a letter on a Monday, Wednesday or Friday in four years. Something was wrong. Terribly, terribly wrong.

CHAPTER

11

B URT WALNUT DELIVERED two, short wraps with his knuckle on Sheriff Fred McNally's open office door. Fred was on the telephone and motioned for Burt to come in and have a seat. Fred hung up the phone.

"How'd you sleep last night, Burt?" asked Fred.

"Got in pretty late. Was that Bob Fields you were talking to?" asked Burt.

"No. It was a town council member. People are concerned that this Olivetti barn fire might have been arson, and therefore homicide. What do you think?"

"I think they might be right," said Burt. "Have you gotten that autopsy report from Bob Fields yet this morning?"

"He says I'll have it this afternoon. After lunch."

"After you left this morning I spent an hour or so with your deputies snooping around Al Olivetti's personal affects. Did you know he owned rental property in the city?"

Fred opened a manila folder on his desk. "One unit at 559 Potomac, and one at 100 Garner."

"Have you sent a deputy up to ask some questions around there yet?"

"Not yet," said Fred. "I have to make contact this morning with the Buffalo PD and get things coordinated."

"Have you heard anything about that mysterious Chevy pickup?"

"Are you worried I forgot how to do my job, you old dog?" asked Fred with a smirk. "Why don't you tell me whether that fire was arson or accidental."

"I got a hunch you're going to find that fire was set. I think that Olivetti fella was dead before it started," said Burt Walnut. "I never known a fella to burn to death in one place unless he was a Buddhist monk. This Italian fella wasn't moonlighting as a Buddhist monk, was he?"

"I can look into it, but I don't think so," said Fred with a chuckle.

Burt Walnut stood up and hooked his thumbs into the pockets of his jeans. "I'm thinking I might go up to the city for some ice cream this morning."

"Is that so?" said Fred. "There wouldn't happen to be any ice cream parlours around 559 Potomac and 100 Garner, would there?"

"I'll get back to you on that," said Burt Walnut with a smile.

"Give me a call after lunchtime and I'll tell you what Bob Fields had to say in his autopsy report," said Fred.

"I'll call if I'm feeling lonely and need somebody to talk to," said Burt, "but I doubt you're gonna tell me much I don't already know. I *would* like to learn how the poor fella did die, though." Burt sauntered out of Fred's office and gave him a backhanded wave over his left shoulder.

Fred sat for a half-minute thumping his pen on his desk, then dialed the phone. "Helen, this is Sheriff McNally, is Bob available to talk? Uh huh. I see. Well, please tell him to call me the minute he's done with that Olivetti autopsy. Thank you, sugar."

CHAPTER

12

T HE GREY, STEEL hydraulic door swung open with a
groan of air as Franklin entered the Buffalo Psychiatric
Centre on Elmwood Avenue Wednesday afternoon. The fluorescent lights droned above his head while his rubber-soled
sandals chirped along the polished white hallway. The walls
were painted a sane yellow and the smell was more sterile and
antiseptic than a normal hospital. No wonder Bernard
requested that Franklin never visit. This place is creepy, he
thought. The receptionist was a bored overweight woman with
a poor complexion who looked as forlorn as the building.

"I'm here to visit a resident," Franklin said.

"I'm sorry?" said the receptionist, phrasing her statement
as a question.

"That's ok," said Franklin. "I'm here to see Franklin."

"First name?" asked the receptionist.

"First name Franklin."

"Ok, last name then."

"Last name Franklin."

"Look sir, we don't have a Franklin Franklin. I know that right off the top of my head."

"No, *I* am Franklin Franklin. I thought you needed my name for your log book or whatever."

"Well I will, but first we need to figure out which resident you are here to see, Mr. Franklin Franklin," said the receptionist with an air of sarcasm.

"Bernard. Bernard Franklin."

"Can I assume you are a relative?" asked the receptionist.

"You should never assume. But yes, he's my brother."

The receptionist shook her head and performed a few deft strokes on her computer keyboard. She picked up the phone and pushed one button, then mumbled something that sounded to Franklin like 'Jews have brown hair.' She asked him to sit in the waiting area. Moments later a hospital administrator appeared through one of the oak double doors that led to the residents' rooms. Franklin thought it was nice that they called them residents, even though they were all there because they were crazy. The administrator was young and very attractive. She introduced herself as Sally Baker and ushered Franklin into a private room.

"Mr. Franklin. May I call you Franklin?"

"Yes," said Franklin.

"Franklin, I am afraid I have to deliver some very difficult news to you."

"Bernard's dead?" asked Franklin.

Sally Baker was completely thrown off her well-rehearsed rhythm. "Yes. Bernard's dead," she said. "Did you already know?"

"No. You bring me into a private room, you tell me you have to deliver difficult news. I couldn't imagine what else you might be preparing to tell me after that setup."

"I am so sorry for your loss, Franklin. Bernard died yesterday morning around 11:30 of his brain tumour.

"*Brain tumour?*" asked Franklin.

"You did know he was sick? Bernard was tested six months ago after complaining of increasingly painful headaches and dizziness. He was told the tumour was inoperable."

"Bernard never told me diddly squat," said Franklin. "He just sent me envelopes full of fingernails. Why didn't the hospital contact me?"

"Bernard has always been a voluntary resident here. He was here of his own volition. Our rules are completely different for contacting next of kin when the resident is not a ward of the state. Only in the event of serious injury or death."

"Or non-payment," offered Franklin.

"Right," agreed Sally Baker. "Or non-payment. Which was never a problem with Bernard. After Bernard died, we tried contacting you by telephone but . . ."

"I don't have a phone," said Franklin.

"Well, yes, we discovered that. We also sent a hospital representative out to your home yesterday but they got lost because there is no such place as Garner Street in the city of Buffalo."

I can thank the multi-pierced lady at the DMV for that one, thought Franklin. He was silent for a moment. "A brain tumour, huh? So Bernard wasn't crazy after all. He had something growing inside his head and nobody found it until it was too late. Did you know he was diagnosed by Dr. Sage Mennox himself?"

"The TV Guru guy?" gushed Sally. "Oh, I just love him. Have you read any of his books?"

"No," said Franklin.

"He's a little unconventional," said Sally. "For instance, we don't refer to our patients as crazy. But when he talks about building a body that is mentally fit and physically strong, I think he's right on target. I've read all his books and I can say that since I started working in a mental hospital— and this is just between you and me—every one of our residents is either unbalanced, unfocused or impure; sometimes all three. Your brother Bernard may have been unbalanced, but he was free to come and go as he pleased."

"He was?" said Franklin in astonishment.

"Of course. This is what I'm trying to tell you. Our policy is completely different for volunteer residents. Bernard would take a long walk every morning and return around lunchtime."

Franklin's bewildered stare was focused on something a thousand miles away. He rested his elbow in his cupped hand and tugged at his upper lip. "I would like to see Bernard now," he said.

"Of course," said Sally Baker. "He's in the morgue. But first

I have some paperwork for you to fill out, and I need to give you this." She removed a white #10 envelope from the pocket of her plum-coloured silk jacket. "It's addressed to you from Bernard."

"What's in it?" asked Franklin. More fingernails, he guessed.

"I don't know," said Sally Baker. "It's addressed only to you."

"Oh," said Franklin. "Silly me. I just thought it might be a good policy to open crazy people's mail. But now that I know Bernard wasn't even crazy, and could come and go as he pleased, you'll have to forgive me for asking such a stupid question."

CHAPTER

13

BURT WALNUT PARKED his silver 1999 Dodge Ram in front of 100 Garner and killed the engine. His visit to the rental property at 559 Potomac had been uneventful. The building was a beige, clapboard, two-storey house with one apartment on each floor. The upper apartment was vacant and in the middle of some renovations. The sink and the toilet had been removed and there was a cardboard box filled with bolts and pipe-fittings on top of a plastic sheet in the middle of the living room. There was also a tool belt, some plumber's wrenches and a large white bucket of plaster.

The ground floor apartment was the residence of seventy-nine-year-old grandmother of fourteen, Emma Stepnoski. She told Burt that she had heard Mr. Olivetti banging around upstairs early Tuesday morning. She said she knew it was him because of all the profanities. "Those Italians have filthy mouths," said Emma. She didn't know where he was headed, but she watched him leave in his truck at around 11:00 a.m.

That information had taken Burt all of seven minutes to solicit. However, he felt obliged to stay another hour drinking coffee, eating fresh-baked lemon cakes and looking at photos of Emma's army of grandchildren.

On the porch at 100 Garner, Burt Walnut met Tommy Balls on his way to work at the 2-4 store. Tommy was wearing a black Korn T-shirt, green fatigue pants and black canvas Converse high tops. The volume in his headphones was loud enough for Burt to hear the unpleasant crackle of modern music through the outside door. Tommy was also high as a kite.

Tommy noticed the old fireman standing on the porch as he checked his mail in the breezeway. Burt nodded with a neighbourly smile and motioned for Tommy to remove his headphones so he could respond to friendly conversation. Tommy complied, but the first stages of pothead paranoia were beginning to creep in. This guy on the porch looks like a cop, Tommy thought. Or worse, someone from my mom's church. He remained in the breezeway with the door closed.

"Hi," said Burt through the glass.

Tommy nodded.

"I see you're checking your mail. You live here?"

Shit, thought Tommy, this guy is a cop. He was beginning to get nervous. He did not want to freak out right there in the breezeway. "What's the problem," asked Tommy. "Are you a cop?"

"No," chuckled Burt. "I'm a fireman. I just want to ask ya

a few questions about your landlord, Mr. Olivetti. Come on out, I won't bite ya."

Tommy's pulse slowly returned to normal. He stuffed his mail into his green army surplus backpack. "I haven't seen Mr. Olivetti," said Tommy. "He's supposed to come fix my sink. It drips."

"Uh huh," said Burt. "Well I don't figure he'll be getting around to that any time soon. He got burned up in a fire at his house last night."

Tommy opened the outside door and stepped onto the porch. "Is he all right?" he asked.

"Nope. He's dead," said Burt.

"Wow," said Tommy.

"*Yeah. Wow*," said Burt Walnut. "When did you last see your landlord?"

"Last week. He was here to cut the lawn. I feel bad and everything, but I'm late for work," said Tommy.

"Uh huh," said Burt. "Who else lives here with you, son?"

Tommy pointed to the windows as he spoke. "There's a nosy old guy who lives in that apartment named Mr. Allspice. And there's a weird fat dude who lives in that apartment named Franklin."

"What makes the fat fella weird?" asked Burt.

"For one thing the dude has got this giant horn that he blows at all hours of the day. It's like one of those Alpine horns that the dudes in the cough drop commercials blow. You haven't heard anything till you've heard that fucking horn blowing through this building. And he's just, like, I don't know, a real hermit. Yesterday he wouldn't even open his door just to hand me a lousy empty pop bottle."

"You don't say," said Burt as he wrinkled his brow and feigned disbelief. He was giving Tommy an audience for his outrageous stories.

"Yeah. He made me yank the bottle through the doorway while the security chain was still attached. For whatever reason, that dude did not want anyone looking inside his apartment last night."

"What'd you need with an empty pop bottle?"

"Nothing. I just needed it, that's all." Tommy's ears began to turn red.

Burt sensed that he had somehow spooked the kid, so he moved on. "About what time was all this nonsense with the pop bottle?" asked Burt.

"Um, it was almost the end of the seventh *Magnum, P.I.* episode, so it had to be just before eight o'clock," said Tommy. "Hey, what's going to happen to this building now that Mr. Olivetti is gone?"

"He has a daughter out west who is coming in to settle his affairs. I'm sure she'll let ya know where things stand with the apartment building and so forth," said Burt. "Well, I've made you late for work. You'd better get going."

Tommy Balls hiked his backpack onto his shoulders and walked off towards the 2-4 store. Damn. Burning to death, thought Tommy Balls. That tops the list of ways I don't want to die. When I go, I hope I'm getting laid and sucking on a fat doobie.

Burt watched Tommy until he was out of view then turned to look inside Franklin's window. He cupped his hands around his eyes and pressed his nose against the dusty glass. That's a mighty small apartment, thought Burt. He noticed the big horn the kid was talking about leaning against an orange vinyl-covered chair. On the table by the window there was a pair of binoculars on top of a pile of newspapers. Burt banged a couple times on the window and an old hound dog popped his head up from behind the coffee table. The dog stretched and made his way over to the window slowly. He blinked his tired eyes up at Burt. One ear was flopped back on top of his head. Burt tapped the glass with his fingernails. "Hey, fella. Ya bite?"

Burt looked around behind him, then turned back to the window. He placed his fingers on the glass and pushed it up easily. He climbed in, closed the window and gave the dog a few gentle pats on the head. The table by the window looked like a good place to start. Wednesday morning's *Buffalo News* local section was folded over to the story about the barn fire at the Olivetti house. Could be a coincidence, thought Burt. He picked up Franklin's binoculars and looked through them at the yellow building across the street, then laid them back on the table.

Franklin's dog climbed up on the couch and settled in for a nap.

Burt walked around the cramped room with his thumbs

hooked in his pockets. He lifted up the end of the alphorn and gave it a good once-over. He blew a little air through it softly and it made a whiny honk. On the wall above the table was a makeshift shrine to the nation of Switzerland. There was a six-foot by four-foot Swiss flag thumbtacked to the wall covered with postcards, magazine photographs, and dangling Alpine bric-a-brac. Burt studied the items briefly, not quite sure how long he had before Franklin's return. On Franklin's twin-sized bed were a grey T-shirt and a pair of tan shorts. He picked them up and smelled them. It was a smell he knew better than any other: smoke. I don't figure this fella was roasting marshmallows by a campfire last night, thought Burt. I'll bet dollars to doughnuts he was roasting his landlord in that tool barn.

Burt gave the dog another pat on the head and left Franklin's apartment through the door. In the foyer, he collided with a surly, red-faced little man, both arms full of groceries.

"Are you the new tenant?" asked Mr. Allspice.

"No sir," answered Burt Walnut.

"Are you a friend of this fat clown?" Mr. Allspice asked, motioning towards Franklin's door with his shiny head.

"No sir, I ain't that neither. My name's Burt Walnut and I'm a Fire Investigator with the Town of Lackawanna. Would you perchance be Mr. Allspice of 2A?"

"I am he," said Mr. Allspice.

"Would you mind if I asked you a few questions," said Burt with a friendly smile.

Mr. Allspice made no effort to cloak his annoyance. "Let me put these bags down," he said as he pushed past Burt and into his apartment. Burt held the door open and followed him in.

"A Fire Investigator, hmm?" said Mr. Allspice, lighting a cigarette. "Do you have any identification?"

Burt showed him his gold Town of Lackawanna Fire Investigator's shield. That seemed to suffice.

"What's this all about?" asked Mr. Allspice.

"I'm regretful to inform you that your landlord Albert Olivetti was killed in a barn fire at his home late last night."

Mr. Allspice's abrasive demeanor softened and he sat down in his chair. "Albert's dead?" Felix Allspice had rented his apartment from Albert Olivetti for thirteen years. He would not have called them friends, but they were definitely acquaintances.

After Felix Allspice's wife died, he sold the house and took the first apartment he looked at. He felt a kinship towards Albert because he too had just lost his wife. As far as the house was concerned, he needed to get away from it. He wanted to forget about the unbearable final months of his wife's stomach cancer. He wanted to forget the doctors, the Hospice people, and even his own family. There was not a room in his house where he could stand and not hear the echoes of his wife's agonizing death moans. After his wife passed away, both his sons and his daughter had asked him to move in with their families.

"This apartment is only temporary," he had said. "Daddy just needs some time to himself."

A year turns into two and on and on, until one day an old fire investigator informs you your landlord is dead and you realize you have been living in the same damned small apartment for thirteen years. Mr. Allspice thought about Albert living alone all those years in his big house. Now he was with his wife. Lucky Albert. He wasn't a bad sort, thought Felix Allspice. But he did rent to some real losers.

"Was that fat oaf next door involved?" asked Mr. Allspice.

"Why do you ask?" asked Burt.

"It just wouldn't surprise me," said Mr. Allspice. "He is a bad element. He is unclean. His mind is unbalanced, unfocused and impure. He's miles and miles down the Road to Crazy. Do you know that he blows a giant horn in that apartment? You have never heard such a racket. I ask you, what sort of person takes up a giant mountain horn as a musical instrument? He keeps all hours. I hear him moving things around over there in the middle of the night all the time. Yesterday morning I heard him banging around in there like he was wrestling a bobcat. Last night I heard a commotion out front and went to see why the porch light was off. I found him packing the trunk of his car."

"You don't say," said Burt. "About what time was that?"

"Just after ten," said Mr. Allspice.

"Pretty late to be packing," offered Burt.

Mr. Allspice lit another cigarette and offered one to Burt. He took it.

"He said he was moving to Switzerland. Switzerland! I told him, good riddance to bad rubbish. That's why I thought you might be the new tenant. I don't know whether to believe that fool or not. For four years it's been like that. Say, you didn't take my *Buffalo News* by chance, did you Mr. ... what was the name again, some sort of fruit?"

"Walnut. Burt Walnut. No sir, I didn't touch your newspaper."

"Walnut? That is an unfortunate name. I don't touch the things myself, break out in hives. Anyway, that fat man-child probably took it—or the dope fiend upstairs. No disrespect to Albert, but he did rent to some real losers. Can you imagine? Moving to Switzerland. That boy has probably never been out of Buffalo!"

"Oh, I don't know," said Burt Walnut, his face obscured by a mist of blue smoke. "I got a feeling he's at least been as far south as Lackawanna."

CHAPTER

14

THE DOCTOR IN the mental hospital infirmary had
Bernard laid out on a steel table, covered up to his neck
by a white bed sheet. Franklin sat on a metal stool beside his
brother's head. They were alone. The smell of Bernard's dead
body was different from the smell of Mr. Olivetti's, though
they had been dead for nearly the exact amount of time.
Bernard smelled more...sanitary. Franklin was cold in just
a T-shirt, shorts and sandals. This is my brother Bernard,
thought Franklin. I am now officially alone in the world.

"I didn't know you were sick. Or that you were free to
come and go as you pleased," said Franklin. "Why didn't you
come visit me? Why didn't you talk to me?" Franklin fiddled
with the corner of the sheet that covered his dead brother
and rubbed the tender bump on his head.

"I've been busy, too, Bernard. I murdered my landlord. I
didn't mean to do it. How it all began would be funny if it
wasn't so terrible. Mr. Olivetti, that's my landlord, whom

you might have met if you ever visited me, came over yesterday morning and wanted the rent. It was almost a month overdue, like it always is, and I didn't have it. I never have it. So he wanted me to do the thing for him. The thing he always wants me to do for him.

"Now Bernard, you know I like girls. I love girls. I loved the girls you used to bring home to our apartment on Ashland. And I especially love teenage girls. I've loved them even before I was a teenager, remember? Remember Rebecca DeLeggio from Grover Cleveland Elementary? In high school, when she became your steady girlfriend, you don't want to know what I did while I was alone and thinking about her in the bubble bath. And Mr. Olivetti must have liked girls too. He was married to one for forty years and they had a daughter together. I don't know what sort of relationship he had with his wife, but it couldn't have been much to speak of.

"Yesterday morning he was in a bad mood and a hurry. He was working on some plumbing or something. He said it was giving him a 'pain in the balls.' He didn't want to argue about the rent, he just wanted me to do my business and be done with it. 'Hurry it up,' he said. 'I have to fix a drip in that pothead's sink.' So I did, Bernard. I did. I got down on my knees, pulled out that dirty guinea's fat cock and worked it like an ice cream cone that was melting in my hands.

"Do you know what I think about when I'm doing that, Bernard? I'll bet you could guess. I think about Switzerland. I imagine that what I'm really blowing is my mighty alphorn as I stand atop a rugged Alpine peak overlooking a Swiss lake. The green hills, they stretch out to the mountains. And the mountains, they disappear into the clouds. Bernard, it must be the closest thing to Heaven on earth.

"Yesterday morning I made a decision. As I knelt on the floor in front of that farting monster, I decided I couldn't live that way anymore. I decided I had to make a change and I had to make it right away. I have always been afraid that Switzerland could never be the place I dream it is. The real Switzerland—the place—with its people and its buildings and its red dirt could never equal my expectations. It could never resemble the vision I have built in my mind since I was a boy. I know that. I'm not a fool. But whatever it is, whatever reality it has to offer, it's better than the hell I endure here in Buffalo. I'm a loser, Bernard. A nobody. I'm a fat, forty-one-year-old footnote. I either need to change my circumstances, or get busy dying.

"So, I made this decision. I decided from that moment on that my life would be different. I mustered all my courage and all my adrenaline and I stood up.

"Bernard, you will not believe what happened next.

"As I rose to my feet, Mr. Olivetti rocked backwards and, like a catapult, threw his head forward and sneezed. He sneezed! His fat chin struck me square in the middle of my head. It was like I'd been walloped with a Louisville Slugger. I fell straight backwards onto my rear. I was seeing tiny starbursts and a rainbow of spots. The collision sent Mr. Olivetti spinning around on his toes until he collapsed onto his back in front of me. His mouth was full of blood and he was mumbling curses at me in Italian. I could tell he was in a lot of pain.

"I scrambled to my knees beside him, 'Are you all right?' I said. His speech was laboured. He was having trouble moving his jaw, and spit out what looked like a tooth. 'I can't move my arms or legs,' he mumbled. There was panic in his eyes. 'What the fuck did you do? You fat fairy. What have you done to me?'

"I said I was sorry, over and over again—'I'm sorry, it was an accident. It's just that I made this decision and...'

"Then his voice took on this sinister tone. 'You're fucked you sonofabitch. I hope you know that. You're not getting away with this. If I die, you're going to fucking fry.' He was staring right at me, Bernard. Then he began coughing and gasping for each breath. 'Sweet Jesus what did you do to me?' he said. 'I'm not going to die—not yet. I can't let you get away with this. I'm going to start screaming until that old buzzard next door comes over to find out what's going on. You're going to jail, you cocksucker. You're going to be sucking cocks for the rest of your miserable life.' Mr. Olivetti started laughing and coughing. He wore a tremendous grin as he considered my fate. Laughing and coughing. It was horrible, Bernard.

"I turned away from him. I couldn't bear to look at him. I knew what I had to do. I picked up my alphorn by the skinny end and twisted my clenched fists tighter and tighter around the boned wood. I didn't believe I could do it. I thought about how many times I would have to hit him before he would be dead. I couldn't bear the thought of it, but I knew I had to kill him, Bernard. I had no other choice.

"The coughing and laughing stopped. I loosened my grip on the alphorn and turned back towards Mr. Olivetti. He was dead. You should have seen the frozen look on his face, Bernard. He was grinning ear-to-ear and his eyes were as big as dinner plates. His last worldly thought was painted on his face: the thought of me going to jail for the rest of my life."

Franklin chuckled at the memory of it. Then he laughed some more. Then he buried his head in his brother's chest and cried like a baby.

He sobbed for several minutes. When he was finished he wiped his eyes and nose on the sleeve of his T-shirt, removed the white #10 envelope from his pocket, and tore it open. Onto Bernard's chest he dumped three fingernail clippings and a small metal key with a rubber grip. He picked up the key and examined it from the end of his nose. It looked like a roller skate key.

"More surprises, Bernard?"

The key had a number engraved inside the window of the rubber grip, 131. It's not a safe-deposit box key, thought Franklin. It's too big and garish for that. Maybe it's a locker key. He tried mentally sliding the key into an assortment of lockers: the airport, the train station, the bus depot, the YMCA. Christ, it could be the key to a locker just about anywhere. "What is this, Bernard? This is what you left for me? A guessing game?"

He sat twirling the miniature key between his stubby fingers. "The bowling alley," said Franklin, nodding his head. The nearest bowling alley was only two blocks north of the Psychiatric Centre on Elmwood Avenue. Franklin recalled Sally Baker saying that Bernard took a walk every morning and returned at lunchtime. Bernard loved to bowl. With a bowling alley so close it was a good guess that that was where he spent his mornings. "What have you got stashed down at the bowling alley, Bernard?"

CHAPTER

15

IT WAS A SLOW Wednesday afternoon at the We-Never-Close, Open 24 Hours convenience store and Tommy Balls' high had worn off. He was sitting on a stool behind the counter, eating free beef jerky and scratching off instant lottery tickets, two of the job's few perks. Tommy reached inside his backpack and pulled out the paperback copy of *Am I Crazy?* by Dr. Sage Mennox. The inscription on the title page read: For Thomas, May you find wisdom in these pages and forever avoid the Road to Crazy. Mom. He fanned through it several times, stopping at random pages to read:

> **Page 154:** If your mind is Impure, you will be easily seduced by sex, violence and addiction. Above all else, Impure Minds are interested in instant gratification. If it is sex the Impure Mind craves, you want it all the time. Your only concern is your own selfish satisfaction. In violence

the Impure Mind always justifies the means by the end result. For instance, on the street, if you want new basketball shoes, you are compelled to kill a boy who owns a pair. Result: you have your new shoes. In the home, if you want a cold beer and a hot meal, you are compelled to hit your wife until she brings them to you. Result: you have your beer and meal. Selfishness is the root of Addiction. Addiction is unique, however, because it encompasses the other two. You can be addicted to sex and violence. The Impure Mind is ruled by Addiction. It feeds the need for constant gratification. Combine these three vices and you are well on your way down the Road to Crazy.

Page 3: Therefore in order to become mentally fit and physically strong you must first be willing to admit that you have done a poor job minding the temple. This process is an inner journey. That is why my book is entitled, *Am I Crazy?* and not, *Are You Crazy?*

Page 259: Crazy people look like everybody else. They are not out wandering the streets in their pyjamas. Crazy people are at your jobs and in your families. Your own mother might be crazy.

"Amen to that, Doc," said Tommy Balls. He closed the book and set it by the register.

Tommy had goals in life, he just thought smoking dope was fun. He wasn't doing it to impress anyone; he mostly smoked alone. And he wasn't doing it to upset his mother, although that was an added bonus. The fact was he enjoyed it. It made him feel good. So what if I enjoy instant gratification, isn't that what this modern world is all about? he thought. Isn't that just a result of our convenience-based society? From the beginning of time, life has been about gratification and convenience. From the discovery of fire and the invention of the wheel to this Open 2-4 store on Forest Avenue in Buffalo. Call it survival or call it convenience, as far as he was concerned the two were interchangeable. Life rewards those who know what they want and take it, he thought. Life is a food chain. The big fish eat the little fish and it's never the other way around. Besides, he thought, I'm only twenty-four years old, I have a lifetime ahead of me to accomplish my goals.

While Tommy was lost in his reverie two gangly white youths, no more than sixteen or seventeen years old, entered the store. They both had eyes that looked like they had been rinsed in chlorine then replaced in their sockets. The tall one checked the mirrors at the end of each aisle while the short one stayed at the door. When the tall one was satisfied the store was empty he pulled a 9mm handgun from the back of his droopy pants and put it in Tommy's face. Tommy nearly fell off his stool. The room was spinning. There was something he was supposed to remember to do. What was he supposed to do? The thief was screaming at him. He looks like a little boy, thought Tommy, except for some curly stubble at the end of his chin and his violet eyes. He's baked! He's stoned out of his mind! Oh God, don't look at him, Tommy thought. You don't want to know what he looks like. Tommy glanced at the door. The short kid had his hands hidden inside the square pocket of his hooded sweatshirt. Look away, Tommy! His eyes darted back to the tall kid with the violet eyes. What is this kid screaming? The thief's voice was coming through to Tommy's ears like gibberish being screamed into a metal drum. Tommy banged opened the register. He grabbed cash in fistfuls and dumped it on the counter. He yanked the plastic organizer out of the drawer and pulled out the cheques and twenty-dollar bills. The thief scooped it all off the counter with his free hand and stuffed it in his jeans pocket.

The short one at the door said something. The tall one turned his head towards the door then looked back at Tommy. Tommy stared into the void—the black circles at the centre of the thief's violet eyes. He recognized the reflection of his own orange goatee and crooked teeth. Oh no! thought Tommy. Oh God!

THERE IS NO REASON for it, thought Tommy as he lay dying behind the counter of the 2-4 store with two bullets in his chest. It doesn't make any sense for me to die. There is just no reason for it.

Little fish might never eat the big fish, thought Tommy as the darkness settled in around him, but little fish are always eating other little fish.

CHAPTER

16

"**WELL, WHAT'S THE VERDICT?**" Burt Walnut asked Fred McNally from a telephone booth in front of Lorenzo's Pizza on West Delavan Avenue in Buffalo.

"You were right," said Fred. "Olivetti was dead before that fire ever started. The coroner said he found no smoke in the lungs. By his best estimate, Olivetti was dead seven hours, maybe more, before he burned in that barn fire."

Burt took a bite of his pepperoni pizza. "What else did he say?"

"He said Olivetti's spinal cord was severed. He broke his neck at the base of his skull, or had it broken for him. Bob also found several broken teeth in his mouth and part of his tongue was bit clean through. His guess for cause of death was some sort of violent, blunt trauma delivered from beneath his chin."

"Ouch," said Burt. "He learned all that from that crispy critter?"

"Bob Fields is good at what he does," said Fred. "We also got a call from the Buffalo PD on the victim's missing Chevy pickup. They found it on the eastside, stripped down and burned out. The plates were gone, but the VIN number matches up. What'd ya find out on your trip to the ice cream parlour?"

"Truth be told, Fred, I think I got our guy right here. He's a tenant in the property at 100 Garner. His name is Franklin Franklin, if you can buy that. I got it off his mail. I got witness reports from the other tenants of him acting suspicious yesterday—banging around his apartment in the morning, not wanting the neighbour to look inside his doorway, packing his car after ten o'clock—stuff like that. I snooped around his apartment a bit, too."

"Aw geez, Burt," groaned Fred.

"Relax, I put everything back where it was. Listen, this fella had a T-shirt and a pair of shorts that smelled like smoke and what was probably turpentine."

"Where are you now?" asked Fred.

"Eatin' my lunch in front of a pizza parlour about four blocks south of the building."

"Go sit on the house in case he comes back. I'll call Buffalo PD and have them meet you with a warrant," said Fred. "What's this fella look like?"

"White, fat, and dopey by all accounts."

BURT DROVE WEST on West Delavan and turned north onto Grant Street. He heard police sirens wailing from what sounded like all directions. In his rearview he saw two Buffalo Police cruisers closing in on his tailgate. He pulled off to the shoulder as they sped by, lights flashing, sirens screaming. Burt got back on the road and tuned his cb radio to the police band. He learned that the Open 24 Hours store on the corner of Grant and Forest had been robbed and that the twenty-four-year-old male clerk was DOA.

"Damn waste," muttered Burt, shaking his head.

He parked a few houses down from 100 Garner on the opposite side of the street and killed the engine. He belched. That pizza wasn't half bad, he thought. He turned the key so he could roll down the automatic window and light a cigarette. The city cops will be here soon, thought Burt. But with any luck, fatso will be here sooner.

CHAPTER

17

FRANKLIN HAD NOT been inside a bowling alley in more than fifteen years. He used to complain when Bernard dragged him along with his girlfriends, then one day Bernard stopped asking. Franklin did not like the smell of bowling alleys. And he did not like the concept of communal shoes. "Buy your own shoes," Bernard would say. Franklin just had no interest in the game.

There were four people on the lanes, two sets of couples. Elmwood Bowl boasted twenty-five lanes on its marquee. Bowling alleys are enormous buildings, thought Franklin. That's probably why they are always so cold. He looked at the numbers on the first bank of lockers he came to, they were all in the 300s. He found locker 131 and turned the key. There was never a doubt.

Inside the locker was a Nike shoebox. He lifted the cover and found a hand-held tape recorder with a Post-It note on it that said, "Play me first," an Altoids breath mint tin, and a folded, brown 9 x 12 catalogue envelope which contained something thick. The box was heavy. He tucked it under his arm and headed out to his car. As he passed the counter, he tossed the miniature key in front of the clerk.

The old clerk was reading the sports section of the Buffalo News. He looked at the key, looked at Franklin, and returned to reading.

Franklin sat behind the wheel of his Pontiac T1000 and placed the shoebox on the passenger seat. He removed the tape recorder and pressed "play."

". . . those crazy bastards, they would have bitten off their fingers if I didn't stop them." Franklin stopped the tape. Bernard had forgotten to rewind. He rewound to the beginning, pressed play, and set the tape recorder on the dashboard.

"Hello Franklin, it's your brother Bernard. I'm dead! It's OK though, I don't mind. Good job finding the locker Franklin— ve-ry cle-ver. I always said you were special. Y'know Franklin, I'm glad I'm dead because now I can tell you my story.

"I'm a crook, Franklin—a big one. I embezzled hundreds of thousands of dollars from Weiner and Fish. Over the years I just skimmed a little off the top of each client's billable hours. I called it Bernard's Share. It's amazing how fast it added up. So why didn't I take the money and run? Why not relocate to some tropical beach and surround myself with luscious strumpets? Because, Franklin, I love Buffalo! It's a great town! Just kidding. About Buffalo, not the money.

"The truth is, Franklin, I really am nuts. I lived out my

final days in a mental institution because I'm fucking crazy! I was in absolute Heaven. I loved the people. I loved the food. I loved the medication. I wouldn't have been happier anywhere else in the world. It was like you and Switzerland, Franklin. Would anything make you happier than waking up every morning and knowing you are in Switzerland? The mental hospital was my Switzerland.

"Seems crazy, huh? It is! Don't fool yourself, little brother, we are all crazy. Everybody has his crazy secrets. Most people spend all day, every day, hiding their crazy secret from the world. Open up the breath mint tin."

Franklin popped open the Altoids breath mint tin. It was filled with fingernails of all sizes.

"How about that, little brother? There must be hundreds of them in there. I collected them from the other mental patients. I told them it was my hobby. My hobby! Those crazy bastards, they would have bitten off their fingers if I didn't stop them.

"So, now we get to the good part, little brother. Open up that envelope. There is $10,000 in there and a passport with your picture in it. Give it a look. Looks just like you, only skinnier I bet. Happy Birthday Mr. Mario Cardone of Philadelphia, PA!"

Franklin could not believe his eyes. He fanned the bills out in front of him. He had never seen so many $100 bills. Franklin scanned the parking lot nervously to see if anyone was watching him.

"There is also a slip of paper in there with a series of letters and numbers written on it. Don't lose it, Chief. That is your new Swiss bank account. If I remember correctly, the balance is somewhere in the neighbourhood of 95,000 bucks. That's a pretty nice neighbourhood. Nicer than Ashland and I'll bet a lot nicer than that dump on Garner. I wish there could be more for you, but I have been indulging my vices for the last few years. All of my vices. I'm sorry I didn't tell you about the money when I was alive, little brother, but it's more fun this way. Besides, you would have made me feel guilty about how much fun I was having. You always had a knack for bringing me down. I hope you were able to get by these last four years without much money. I, for one, had a blast. A blast!

"I'm dead now, Franklin. I've been dying for a while. They tell me I have a tumour in my brain the size of a racquetball. 'Cancer of the noggin' just like mom used to say. I knew I was dying long before they told me, before the headaches became too much for me to bear. A man knows when he's dying.

"Listen to me Franklin—I mean, Mr. Cardone. Get in your car—do you still have that Pontiac?—and drive straight to the airport. Start a new life. Go to Switzerland, little brother. Pack your big horn and buy a one-way ticket. This is my parting gift to you. But listen to me Franklin. This is your brother Bernard speaking to you from the other side. Go to Switzerland and be happy if that's what you want. But if I can give you one piece of advice to make your remaining time on Earth more livable, it's this: always remember that it doesn't matter if you live in a small apartment or a mansion on a hill. It doesn't matter if you live in a mental institution or on a beach in St. Croix. It's all in your mind, Franklin. Happiness is a state of mind. Bon voyage, little brother. Go find your happiness."

The wheels in the tape turned mechanically for a few moments until the player clicked off. Franklin slouched back into a fog of disbelief. He looked into his own eyes staring back from his new passport photo: Cardone, Mario. Philadelphia, PA. He was Italian now, just like Mr. Olivetti. I have never owned a passport, he thought. It just never came up. Franklin's eyes were raw and watery. A tear streaked down his face and he caught it on his cheek with a hundred-dollar bill.

He was exhausted. So much about the last two days was just too much to absorb. And now the idea of waking up tomorrow in Switzerland was enough to make him lose sphincter control. That sonofabitch Bernard, he thought. He drummed his fingertips on the steering wheel then head-butted the centre of it. The horn blew.

"Yo! Blow it out your ass, fatso," said a high school kid as he walked with his date through the parking lot past Franklin's car.

It's not safe to be sitting here, Franklin thought. He hustled everything back into the shoebox and started the engine. If I'm leaving tonight, thought Franklin, I have to do two things first: pack my alphorn, and let out my dog. He pulled out of the parking lot and headed south on Elmwood towards 100 Garner.

CHAPTER

18

INSIDE FRANKLIN'S STUDIO apartment at 100 Garner
Street, Burt Walnut and three Buffalo Police officers sat
waiting for Franklin's return. It was dusk. The lights were
off inside the apartment, but there was enough light coming through the window to see around the room. One officer sat on Franklin's orange chair on the side of the table
furthest from the window. The second officer sat by the
door on a black metal folding chair he found leaning against
the refrigerator—apparently intended for company. The
third officer was reclined on one elbow on Franklin's bed.
Burt Walnut was seated on the couch, petting Franklin's
hound dog.

The cops had told Burt all about the homicide scene at the
2-4 store. They noted the coincidence of the victim being
Franklin's upstairs neighbour. Burt told them he had spoken
with the boy that morning in connection with the arson—now
homicide—investigation. The four men exchanged thoughts

about the tragedy of a young man being gunned down in the prime of his life, a reality they had all witnessed far too often. The thieves had made off with $177. The young suspects had already been apprehended; they lived around the corner from the 2-4 store. They told police they were just trying to score some cash to get high. When the tall one was asked why he killed the clerk, even after he had complied and given him all the money, he responded, "I don't know."

I don't know. That was an answer that seemed to cover a lot of ground in this modern world. Burt sat meditating silently on that very thought. Mr. Allspice's phone was ringing next door and no one was answering.

THREE HOURS PASSED. Now it was dark both outside and inside the apartment. Once in a great while a car would roll past and for an instant illuminate the room. The men readied themselves for the possibility that the car might stop to park, but none did.

For the fifth time in three hours Mr. Allspice's phone rang at least a dozen times. Burt was chewing on that. It had really begun to bother him. Franklin's dog was snoring on Burt's lap. He got up and straightened his blue jeans then nodded to the officers in the room.

"Piss break?" asked the cop at the door.

"Actually," said Burt, "I'm going over to check on that neighbour. That ringing phone is aggravating me. He's an old-timer and I don't know where else he'd be at this hour but in his apartment."

Burt stepped into the foyer and knocked on 2A.

"Mr. Allspice? Mr. Allspice, it's Burt Walnut the Fire Investigator. Everything all right in there?"

Burt went out to the porch and pressed his nose against Mr. Allspice's window. The television was on and Mr. Allspice was sitting in his easy chair with a hardbound copy of *Am I Crazy?* by Dr. Sage Mennox open on his lap. His eyes were open wide and bright in the light of the television. Burt banged on the window and called to him.

"Mr. Allspice! Mr. Allspice! Felix!"

At that point the three Buffalo Police officers were at Franklin's window and had thrown it open.

"What's going on, Burt?"

"Call an ambulance," said Burt. "I think this old-timer is dead in his chair."

THE WHOLE NEIGHBOURHOOD was out on their porches or down in the street when the paramedics wheeled Felix Allspice's dead body into the ambulance in front of 100 Garner. Little 101 and her mother were on their stoop, wearing thick socks and fuzzy bathrobes. Burt overheard one of the paramedics tell a Buffalo cop that Mr. Allspice had most likely suffered a massive stroke, but they could not know for sure until an autopsy was performed. Allowed too much stress into his life, thought Burt.

Burt was standing next to Mr. Allspice's easy chair. He looked at his watch: 10:05. With all the action in the street, Burt and the cops had given up hope on Franklin returning to his apartment. Even a fat mope would be spooked by all this commotion, they reasoned. They decided to let an unmarked car sit on the house overnight.

What sort of fella leaves their dog to fend for himself, thought Burt? I don't care if you are a murdering, fire-starting, sonofabitch. A man's got no soul who leaves his dog behind.

One of the paramedics returned to Mr. Allspice's apartment to shut off the lights and seal the door.

"Oh, I didn't know there was still someone in here," said the paramedic. "Are you the partner of the deceased?"

"Hell, no!" said Burt a bit flustered. "I'm Burt Walnut, Lackawanna Fire Investigator."

"You're who?"

"Christ, I stood right over you while you were pounding this fella's chest and filling him with rubber tubes," said Burt.

"Oh. I didn't recognize you."

"Go on ahead," said Burt. "I'll close everything up."

Burt lit a cigarette and walked over to Mr. Allspice's bookshelves. From the photographs, Burt surmised that Felix Allspice had quite a large family. He was married. He served during the war, in the Marines. His wife was a handsome woman at one time. All these pictures of smiling family faces, thought Burt. Why would an old man elect to live alone like this?

The telephone rang. Burt lifted an eyebrow and looked at it. He wondered if it was one of the smiling faces that he would have to break the news to. It rang again and he picked up.

"Hello?" said Burt.

"Mr. Allspice?" The connection sounded distant and canned, like Billy Browski's cellular phone.

"Who is calling?" asked Burt.

"Is this Mr. Allspice? Do I have the right number?"

Well at least it's not a family member, thought Burt. He cleared his throat, "This is the Allspice residence, go ahead."

"Is this Mr. Allspice?" The connection was fading in and out.

"This is his, uh, brother . . . Burt," said Burt Walnut.

"Oh. Well Burt, this is Franklin, Mr. Allspice's next door neighbour. Could you give him a message for me?"

Sonofabitch, thought Burt. "I, um . . . I suppose I could do that."

"Tell Mr. Allspice that I would appreciate it if he would watch my dog for me. Can you tell him that, Burt?"

"Well where will you be, Franklin? Where can he reach you?"

"Tell him that my door is locked, but that my window pushes open easily. He just needs to open it and the dog will come out."

"This is a most unusual request," said Burt as he looked frantically out the door and window. Everyone had gone. "Can you leave a number where you can be reached? How long will you be gone?"

"Tell Mr. Allspice I would appreciate it if he could do me this one favour. I know we don't get along, but I don't think he has anything against my dog. Tell him he can destroy my alphorn as payment. He can burn it if he wants."

"I'm sure he'll want to know how to contact you, Franklin. Can't you give me a number or an address where you can be reached?" Burt was beginning to sound desperate and he knew it.

"I have to go now," said Franklin.

"Wait!" cried Burt. "Wait!"

The line was silent for a moment.

"What?" asked Franklin.

The vein in Burt's forehead was a split second from breaking the skin and spraying all over Mr. Allspice's living room. He was strangling the receiver with all his might. Reluctantly, Burt allowed all his bottled-up pressure to flow out through his nostrils. His shoulders sagged and his eyes rolled towards the ceiling.

"What's the dog's name?"

"Bernard," said Franklin. Then the line went dead.

CHAP+ER

19

FRANKLIN REPLACED THE air phone into the seat in front of him. He slid the long distance card he bought at the airport gift shop into the pocket of his brand new Gap cotton chinos and reclined into his leather first-class seat. He looked out the window but saw only darkness. He knew he was somewhere over the Atlantic.

"Would you care for a beverage, sir?" asked the pretty blonde flight attendant.

"Do you have Moxie cola?" asked Franklin.

"No sir, we don't have that."

"Do you have rum?"

"Yes. We have Bacardi."

"I'll have rum, hold the coke please. And no ice, thank you."

"Do you prefer light or dark rum, sir?" asked the flight attendant.

"Yes, that would be fine. Both please. Thank you," said Franklin.

The flight attendant handed a plastic cup and two tiny bottles of rum over the gentleman seated next to him. He placed the potables in his lap. I know this guy next to me, he thought. Franklin had been wracking his brain since he boarded the plane. His mind was just too tired to think. He turned and looked again at his seatmate. The tan, bald head. The black eyebrows. Even the way he dressed seemed familiar. Franklin did not notice that his staring was making the man uncomfortable.

"Yes," said the man. "It's me."

"It's who?" asked Franklin.

"Oh, I'm sorry," the man blushed. "I thought you recognized me."

"I think I do," said Franklin.

The man extended his hand. "Dr. Sage Mennox."

"*Am I Crazy?* by Dr. Sage Mennox," said Franklin. "The TV Mental Guru guy. I'm Frank—Mario Cardone. Pleased to meet you."

"That's me. Pleased to meet you, too."

Awkward silence.

"You ever drink Moxie cola?" asked Franklin.

"I'm afraid I've never heard of it," said Dr. Mennox.

"Been around since the 1800s. Used to be more popular than Coca-Cola. Tastes sort of like carbonated medicine. It's good, though. I think now they only sell it in New England and upstate New York."

"Sounds fine," said the doctor.

Franklin decided that was sufficient for polite small talk. "I've got to tell you Doc, you diagnosed a close friend of mine four years ago. If I recall correctly, I believe the term you used for his condition was 'Nuts.' Is that a proper medical term? Anyway, you said without immediate care he would continue down the Road to Crazy."

The doctor immediately felt uncomfortable. He wondered if he could flag the flight attendant and ask for a seat change. "Four years ago? He must have been one of the last patients I saw in private practice. What was his name?"

"Bernard Franklin." Franklin dumped his rums into his plastic cup.

Dr. Mennox tried desperately to recall the case, but his mind drew a complete blank. He had done little more than write, speak, and make television appearances for the last four years. He tried to make eye contact with the flight attendant. "I'm embarrassed to say I don't recall the case. How is your friend?"

"He died yesterday morning of a brain tumour. Inside a mental institution." Franklin drank his rums in one swallow.

"Stewardess!" cried Dr. Mennox. "Stewardess. Over here."

"We ask that you please address us as 'flight attendants,' sir," said the pretty blonde.

"Relax, Doc, I'm not crazy," said Franklin. "I'm just making conversation."

"Could I move to another seat?" asked Dr. Mennox. "This one seems to be broken."

"I'm sorry sir," said the flight attendant. "This is a full flight. What seems to be the trouble with your seat?"

"Oh, never mind," said Dr. Mennox. "Just bring me a double vodka martini, neat. With onions, not olives."

"And a couple more rums," added Franklin, tapping his cup. "What sends you to Switzerland, Doc?"

Dr. Mennox was delighted with the change of subject. "I am speaking in Geneva at an international summit on mental health."

"Kudos to you," said Franklin as he toasted the doctor with his empty plastic cup. "Now tell me what you think of this for mental health."

Oh God, thought Dr. Mennox, here comes the shit-storm.

"Yesterday morning I made a decision. I decided I wanted to live a better life. As it turns out, circumstances have allowed me to embark on that life. So, before I got on this plane I was on my way home to pack my one prized possession. I was driving along in my Pontiac and thinking to myself, Frank—Mario, why not start sooner than later? It's high time for you to make a clean break. Start over from scratch. Square one. Ground zero. So, I turned the car around, headed to the mall, bought some new clothes, and got on a plane to Switzerland. What do you think of that, Doc?"

"Are you getting a new dog in Switzerland?"

"What?" said Franklin.

"I'm sorry, but I couldn't help overhearing while you were on the telephone that you neglected to make arrangements for your dog before embarking on this new life. I assume that he was your one prized possession."

"Well you should never assume, Doc. Because that's when you make an ass out of you and me."

Franklin thought he would let the good doctor chew on that nugget of knowledge for a while. For all the lousy advice this guy has to offer, thought Franklin, a dose of wisdom from Miss Parson at Grover Cleveland Elementary might serve him well. Franklin bent his face into that impish smile that Little 101 had complimented him on and turned back towards the window.

The flight attendant returned with the drinks.

Dr. Mennox leaned back and sipped his martini. He also could not help overhearing that the man seated next to him was named Franklin on the telephone, yet referred to himself as Mario. Whether or not he wished to admit it, he was miles and miles down the Road to Crazy. With all the lonely nuts out there I'll never go out of business, thought Dr. Mennox. He looked at his gold Rolex. They would be landing in three hours. With any luck, this fat nut next to me will get drunk and pass out, he thought. He finished his martini with a gulp and tried like hell to avoid eye contact.

ABOUT THE AUTHOR

Chris Millis wrote the screenplay for *Small
Apartments*, which made its World Premiere at the
2012 South By Southwest Film Festival in Austin,
Texas. Millis is a prize-winning, bestselling author,
producer, screenwriter, and cartoonist. He divides his
time between Los Angeles and Upstate New York
where he lives with his wife and identical twin sons.